THE OCCUPANT

THE AFTERLIFE INVESTIGATIONS #3

AMBROSE IBSEN

1

U p to this point in my life, I'd never hitchhiked. It'd been one of those things my mother had always warned me about. One was likely to end up in Buffalo Bill's backseat, in Jack the Ripper's windowless van, she'd maintained.

Of course, when you're wandering down the long, empty roads of the Upper Peninsula near dawn, you haven't got much choice but to hike your thumb out.

Some miles into our wandering, our bodies chilled by the rain, Jake and I were picked up by a kindly gentleman, about sixty years old, who was on his way to the lower half of Michigan to visit his grandkids. He flashed his lights at us and wheeled his SUV to the right side of the road. He took a quick look at us in his side mirror before unlocking his doors. I don't know what criteria he used in picking up hitchhikers, but it seemed we passed his sniff test. It helped that the two of us looked pathetic, our clothes and hair matted against our bodies like we were drowned rats.

"Car trouble?" asked the man as we sidled up to the side of the SUV.

A co-ed possessed by an entity from beyond the world of the dead had torched my Cavalier and everything in it. I supposed that such things, rare though they are, fell beneath the umbrella of 'car trouble', and I gave him a nod.

"Where are you headed?" he asked. He had a toothpick in his mouth and was listening to something loud and jazzy. Despite my fatigue, I recognized the playing of the Wynton Kelly Trio and had to stifle a laugh. Hearing bits and pieces of *Smokin' at the Half-Note* streaming out of this guy's window in the middle of Nowhere, Michigan, was surreal to me.

Jake gave the man a puppy dog look that said, "We'll go anywhere warm and dry," and before we knew it the guy was waving us in. He didn't mind that our rain-soaked clothing would dampen his interior—the back of the SUV, it turned out, had been well-worn by an energetic little dog, a beagle bewilderingly named 'Peanuts'—and asked that we make ourselves at home. He offered to drive us to the nearest highway rest stop, offered to let us use his cell phone, and even bought Jake and I a meal and a hot coffee once we got there.

Jake and I said as little as we could get away with while sitting in the back seat of the SUV. Wynton Kelly tickled the ivories, Peanuts the beagle wandered between my lap and Jake's, and I tell you, petting that dog was the only comfort either of us had known for a good, long while. The driver, whose name I learned was Derrick, asked us a few questions about our travels, talked about the weather, but wasn't bothered when we gave him half-formed answers.

I spun him some yarn about how we'd been planning to go camping. I mentioned the car fire, but acted bewildered as to its source, and then cracked a joke about how I'd just put new tires on the thing.

"You'd be surprised," said Derrick as he navigated the winding roads. "A lot of abandoned cars in these parts. The UP... it's a place where things, and people, sometimes come for the express purpose of getting lost." The trees cast the pavement in dense shadow. The sun was playing hard to get and had been doing so since dawn. Now and then it would peer out from behind the shield of rainclouds in the sky, only to duck back into the mess of grey. I swear, the sky as glimpsed through the sunroof looked like Rembrandt's *Storm on the Sea of Galilee.* Judging by his carefree inflection, Derrick hadn't meant anything with that remark—he was just making conversation.

But Jake and I shuddered all the same.

We'd come looking for something long-abandoned to these dense woods—a mining town largely vacated in the 1870's called Milsbourne. It was there we'd hoped to find some answers to our numerous questions. Questions that had brought us all the way from the Chaythe Asylum, out of Ohio, and into remote northern Michigan.

The search for those answers looked like it was going to cost us everything, though.

Jake looked shell-shocked. He palmed at his cell phone every now and then, staring down at it with a tremulous fear that plagued his hands and throat, but didn't so much as switch it on. He'd gotten a text from Elizabeth—from the monstrosity lurking within her—and just hadn't been the same since.

It'd been an invitation. Or, perhaps, a *challenge.*

Won't you join me in Milsbourne?

The beastly thing was on to us—had been for a while—and had thought nothing of destroying the car to leave us stranded.

But it hadn't killed us.

It could have overpowered us both as we fled through the woods, scared out of our wits, but was content to simply frighten. Why had that been? What did it want to show us in forgotten Milsbourne?

Derrick let us out at the rest stop, fixed us up with a pair of large coffees and a breakfast at the adjacent McDonald's, and then set off. I thanked him profusely, could have hugged the man like he was my own father, and then Jake and I set about demolishing the food before us in the well-lit dining area. Our clothes had begun to dry, leaving the fabric starchy in places and the skin beneath wrinkled.

When the food was gone, we had no choice but to face the elephant in the room, to turn our harried minds to other matters that, even in the daylight hours, made our blood run cold.

"Where do we go from here?" asked Jake. The food had brought his color back, and he sucked down the hot coffee, black, in an effort to regain some of the warmth he'd lost on our rainy death march.

I looked past him, spying my haggard reflection in the window. My hair was sticking up in frizzy cowlicks and I looked like I was wearing eye black. "I dunno," I replied. "Maybe we should run out there, try and flag down Derrick. Hanging out with him and his grandkids sounds damn fine compared to sticking around here."

Jake rolled his eyes. "No, seriously. What happens now that... that Elizabeth has made it to Milsbourne?" His girlfriend's name—*Elizabeth*—left his lips without the usual loving affection. He said it almost phonetically, like he was trying to pronounce the scientific name of some venomous snake, and I couldn't blame him. "Are we too late?"

I plucked the lid off of my coffee and stared down into the pool of black. The steam rose up and washed over my face as I took a sip. "Nah. We're not too late. At least, I don't think we are. That thing led us here, but it's not through with us yet. It wants us to meet it in Milsbourne. Until we find the old ghost town, until it meets us face-to-face there for some kind of final showdown, this won't end."

"This isn't some kind of action movie," he pleaded. "What final showdown could this thing possibly want? It could have killed us a hundred times by now. Once it wrecked the car it could have snapped our heads off, no problem."

I nodded. "Yup. Which means it's still got something in store for us and is waiting until we hike into Milsbourne to reveal it. Don't ask me what." I balled up my hash brown wrapper and made a free-throw into a nearby garbage can. I missed. "As to what's next, that's a tough question. We're going to need some help. We've got no supplies, no map, no car." I held out my palm. "Let me see your phone."

Jake handed it to me with obvious reticence. His flush cheeks sank into a frown and his youthful eyes, darkened by a lack of sleep, narrowed on the device's unlit screen. "What are you gonna do?"

I switched on the phone and watched it power up completely before answering him. When all systems were go and there were no more ominous text messages waiting for us from the Occupant, I flagged down a woman in a McDonald's uniform and asked her if she knew the address. Jotting it down on a napkin, I dialed 4-1-1 and waited for an operator to answer. "There's someone who may be able to help," I told him, rapping upon the tabletop with my fingers.

2

Jane Corvine was *not* happy to hear from me.

At the sound of my voice—at my very utterance of "Hello"—she'd barked into the phone like a pit bull raring to maul a mailman. I held my ground, though. "Jane, I'm not calling you to catch up, I'm calling because it's *important*. Things are happening and we need your help. There's no one else I can turn to in this."

The woman seethed. "I seem to remember telling you that I never wanted to hear from you again. I suppose I owe you a bullet for this phone call, don't I? How did you even get this number?"

I ignored her and pressed on. "I'm calling about the Occupant," I stressed. "It's on the move."

Jane scoffed. "No shit. And I'll bet it hitched a ride in that student of yours, didn't it?" Jane had warned me about the possibility of Elizabeth falling under the Occupant's sway. There was no pride in her voice as she said it—no "*I told you so.*" "What's happened, then?"

"It led us all the way up here, to Michigan," I explained. "But there's more. It seems to be gearing up for something.

I've learned a few things since we last spoke and I want to touch base with you. If anyone can help us stop this thing, it's you." I paused. "I wouldn't call you without a good reason. The Occupant is about to get what it wants unless we move. Quickly."

For what seemed an eternity, Jane weighed my words. Finally, she conceded. "All right. I'll give you an address where we can meet. Where you coming from?"

I couldn't help but snicker. "Actually, it's funny you ask. We're experiencing a bit of car trouble, so... I was wondering if maybe you could—"

"Jesus," she muttered. "Well, where are your asses at, then? And who's with ya? You keep saying 'we'. Who's tagging along, and can we trust them?"

"Oh, it's one of my students, Jake. The Occupant took a liking to his girlfriend. He's fine. No worries there."

Jane grumbled. She didn't sound too thrilled about involving another outsider in this affair—either that, or she was still pissed about having to drive out to pick us up. "OK, and where are you now?"

I gave her the address to the rest stop and let her do a bit of mental math.

"All right. I'll be there in about an hour," she answered. And then she cut the line.

"Is she coming?" asked Jake.

I nodded. "Should be here within an hour." I reclined in my seat, had a look around the restaurant, and wondered if I could get away with a discrete nap while waiting for our ride. My head was beginning to pound and the caffeine wasn't doing anything for me anymore. My feet, too, were mighty sore, and my shoes were still damp. "When she gets here," I added, "don't talk to her unless you have to, all right? She doesn't like to chat. Not a very friendly lady."

Jake took his orders and busied himself by getting rid of the trash on our table. With that, he plopped down in the chair beside me and we watched the rain fall through the window, nodding off intermittently while waiting for Jane to show up. Eventually she did, pulling up to the restaurant in a black pickup.

She rolled her window down a touch, peering in at us from the parking lot.

I nudged Jake awake. "She's here."

We set out into the rain to meet her.

"TELL ME EVERYTHING," she demanded. "Every last detail."

Jane's truck was a dingy thing. Once, probably, it'd been a top of the line truck, but one too many rainy days with the windows open had left the leather interior thoroughly cracked. There was a smell in the cabin that was hard to trace—something between wet dog and warmed-over skunk —but there weren't any animals inside I could blame it on. The ash tray up near the steering wheel was crammed with spent butts.

Before regaling her with everything I'd learned since our last meeting, I forced her to surrender one of her precious Marlboro Reds, and took several puffs while trying to get my thoughts straight.

I told her about how I'd found Jake, left in a daze after being attacked by Elizabeth. I told her about our meeting with Elizabeth's parents—both the queer call we'd gotten while there, and what we'd learned of Elizabeth's true heritage. She was a Lancaster, like Enid had been, and had apparently been born in Michigan near a small ghost town called Milsbourne. The name of the town meant nothing to

Jane, which surprised me. I then told her about our trip to the university library, where we'd discovered her uncle, the notorious W. R. Corvine, had checked out—and never returned—the only book in the library's extensive catalog that dealt with Milsbourne. From there, I covered our consultation with professor John Prince, who'd shared with us some tidbits about a fellow academic, Jamieson Monroe, who'd gone looking for the ghost town out of scholarly interest and had ended up finding something there that'd ruined his previously ironclad mind.

"All roads are pointing to Milsbourne," I said. "With general directions provided by John Prince, we set out for the UP and arrived here yesterday evening. The Occupant messed with us all the while. It showed up on the side of the road, in the woods... We were close to Milsbourne, and were going to set out into the forest at first light in search of it, when the Occupant lured us away from the car. We were very nearly lost in the woods, and when we found our way out, we discovered my car on fire. Everything in it— including the map where I'd marked down Milsbourne's coordinates—was lost in the blaze. We had to hitchhike to this rest stop and the rest is history."

Jane listened with a deep-set grimace, hands balanced atop the wheel. Raking a hand through her short, blonde hair, she appeared at a loss for words. It turned out I was mistaken, though, because she promptly replied, "You two fucked up."

"Yeah, as if I wasn't aware of *that*," I muttered, putting out my cigarette. "Now the question is, what's waiting for us in Milsbourne? How does an old mining town play into this? Your uncle looked into Milsbourne, seemed to have an interest in it. Did he say why? Did he ever mention the place?"

She shook her head. "Never breathed a word of it to me. I wasn't his secretary, you know. He told me what he wanted me to know, but he didn't leave behind a detailed outline of all he knew." She rubbed at her temples, clenching her jaw against a jolt of fear or annoyance—I couldn't tell which. "Might be something in those papers you took from the cabin. Did you look through them?"

"The ones that went up in flame along with the car?" I chuckled. "We leafed through them before coming up north. There wasn't anything related to Milsbourne in them that we could find, no. But if there was, it's gone now."

"The research is gone, too, huh?" She looked ready to spit. "Of course it is. Why wouldn't it be?" With a sigh, she added, "I told you I never wanted to see you again, and I meant it."

"Well, why'd you show up, then? Why pick us up?" I shot back. "It's because you want to wipe this thing off the face of the planet too, am I right? So, let's cut the shit and get moving. We need to find out where Milsbourne is at. I feel like the Occupant has been trying to lure us out there. I don't know why, but it didn't attack us, didn't *kill* us, when it had the chance. That must mean it wants us to do something for it. Something that can only be realized in Milsbourne. What do you think?"

"I think we're up Shit Creek with no paddle," she uttered. Looking out the rain-flecked window and fogging it up with a heavy sigh, she continued. "I know the area you were poking around in. I know of the mines, the hills. Of course, that doesn't mean I know just where this old town is at. There are a lot of towns buried out there in the trees, you know? In order to find the right one, we're going to have to do some digging, ask around, and find someone who knows their shit."

There was then a brief silence, which Jake pounced on and promptly broke like a porcelain vase. "What are we going to do once we find Elizabeth?" he asked, the edge in his voice betraying hope. "How can we save her?"

Jane turned to look at him, sent him a gaze of ice that left him withering against his seat. "I'll tell you what we're going to do," she said, pointing at her forehead. "I'm going to put a bullet 'tween her eyes."

3

I had no supplies, no map. I didn't even have a car, or a fresh change of underwear.

Even if we managed the best case scenario—that of rescuing Elizabeth, sending the Occupant back to where it came from and returning to Moorlake in time for classes, I was still majorly *fucked*. I didn't have the money to replace my old beater and wasn't even sure that I could buy a cheeseburger without my credit cards bumping their limits. I'd spent a lot of money over the past several days without thinking about it, purchasing necessities. But when all was said and done, if I didn't end up dying beforehand, I was set to face another nightmare—that of utter poverty—upon my return home.

Now wasn't the time to worry about that, of course. We were still trying to figure out that "survival" thing and I realized it probably wasn't a good idea for me to get my hopes up on that front. Any fears I had that were contingent on my survival were pretty damn premature.

After a lot of hemming and hawing, Jane took us to her place. She lived on a remote stretch of land several miles from the dirt road that had first led me to her uncle's cabin, in a weatherbeaten double-wide. Jane Corvine was not used to having guests, it soon became clear. She had to move a bunch of crap out of her living room to make space for us, and when that was through she offered us the sofa and recliner to crash on.

But first she ordered us to shower.

Jake and I took turns using the cramped shower stall in her bathroom, dashing on flowery soaps and shampoo which—under the circumstances—smelled incredible when compared to the reek of the road we'd brought with us. Jane threw our clothes in the dryer and when the two of us were reasonably clean and fresh she broke into her stock of Wonder Bread and whipped us up a pair of PB & J's.

"Just like mom used to make," I declared as I dug in.

Jane wasn't in a joking mood, though. She was elsewhere, marching through the trailer, room to room, as if searching for something. She finally found it in her bedroom—a black handgun. I don't know what kind—I don't know a thing about firearms—but judging by its size I didn't doubt that a single shot from it would probably knock a man's head from his shoulders. She placed it in a shoulder holster and zipped a jacket up over it.

"What's that for?" I asked, eyeing her suspiciously.

"When you're rooting around in the trash you need to take precautions to protect yourself from the junkyard dogs," she replied, as if that was any way to answer. "I'm going into town."

"What for?" asked Jake, the sandwich sticking to the roof of his mouth and making his voice slurred.

"Gonna try and find me someone who knows about this town, Milsbourne. I think I know a guy who might be able to help. He's lived here all his life, does a lot of hiking." She stepped into a pair of black boots and sat down to lace them. "You two need to stay here. Get some rest. You're useless to me if you're half-asleep."

She was right, of course. "You know," I began, "I've been seeing things. Terrible things. I told you, while we were heading up north, the Occupant kept popping up. Sometimes it was close, seemed real—other times I thought I was just losing my mind. It's hard to know what's real, but I think the paranoia's been getting to me."

Jane crossed her legs, munching on a heel of bread. "It may not be paranoia at all," she replied. "Else I've been paranoid for decades now." The bread didn't seem like it was going to go down easily, and she chased it with a glug of tap water. "I'll be honest with you, I had a dream last night— longer and more vivid than any I'd had in years—of the Occupant." She nodded, gaze growing a bit distant. "I get them sometimes. After that thing has lived in your head, you can't help but have flashbacks now and then. It never leaves you. Remember how I told you that? But... last night, I was sleeping in my bed. Woke up out of a dead sleep to find the thing standing in the corner of my room. It didn't have a body, or even a real shape to it. It was just like a shadow, but... the eyes... the mouth... they were there. I never had the least doubt of what I was looking at. And it just stood there, real still, like a statue, watching me as I slept. Watching and watching. I about jumped out of my skin, but I told myself the same thing you did. 'It's a dream. It's paranoia.' Well, when I next opened my eyes, it was standing right next to me, closer than you are now, and was just staring straight down at me. Those eyes... those *holes* it's got, through which you can see the world beyond, they were all over me, rummaging around in my mind, my soul, even though it never laid a hand on me. When I got out of bed this morning... when I felt brave enough to get out from beneath the covers, I suspected something was going on. I'm not surprised you called, honestly."

Jake set his half-eaten sandwich down on his paper plate and spent some time glancing about the room, no doubt searching for that ominous shadow figure Jane had described.

I'd heard enough of her dream-borne horrors and changed the subject to something I felt was more action-able. "What's the connection between Enid and Elizabeth? They have the same last name—Lancaster. Do you know any Lancasters? Are they associated with Milsbourne, maybe?"

Jane didn't have an answer and just shrugged. "Maybe. I guess we'll see. Truth be told, though my uncle talked about how much the Occupant liked her, how it could have grown in her, he never told me where he'd met Enid. Maybe she was in the asylum already and he just found a good subject in the pool of crazies available to him there." She started for the door. "But if the Occupant has taken hold of Elizabeth in this way, then it's getting ready to emerge into the world." She shot me a knowing glance.

"It's going to use her—going to use her womb so that it can be born into the world, right?" I asked.

She nodded. "If things have gone this far, I can only imagine that the Occupant has everything it needs and is running to Milsbourne to let the bun in its oven grow." Glancing at Jake, she arched a silver brow. "Did you fuck her recently?"

I admit, Jake and I both blushed.

"Did you fuck the girl?" repeated Jane.

Jake was evasive, but eventually answered in the affirmative. "Well, yeah..."

"Well, I hope you enjoyed it, because you may have just given the thing exactly what it wanted." Jane picked up her keys and prepared to leave.

"Hold up," blurted Jake. "Just because Elizabeth has come to Michigan, that doesn't necessarily mean that... that she's pregnant." He looked to me, something pleading in his gaze. "The other girl, Enid, tried running from the asylum. Maybe she was headed to Milsbourne, too, right? But was *she* pregnant?" He ended on a high note, like he'd just pulled off some clever checkmate, but Jane was quick to offer a gruff reply.

"As a matter of fact, she was."

I got out of my chair and choked down the bite of sandwich in my mouth. "Wait, Enid was pregnant? You didn't say anything about that the last time we spoke. You said that things hadn't progressed that far."

Now it was Jane's turn to blush. She gave a weak shrug, like her omission was no big deal. "I didn't see what it mattered. In Enid's case, nothing came of it. She was struck down by my uncle before she could escape, so what did it matter?"

"Fine, but who was the father?" I asked. Though, truthfully, I already had a suspicion.

Jane leveled her steely gaze on me and shook her head in disbelief. "What, can't you guess?" She bit her lower lip and then turned back towards the door. "He let slip that he'd decided to give it a try... because the Occupant asked him to, of course."

"Dr. Corvine? He... he impregnated Enid?" asked Jake.

If that was truly the case, then there was a whole new face on the matter. The Occupant had been very close to getting what it wanted back in 1989. Had it not been for Corvine's interference on the night of the Third Ward Incident, the entity would have scored its much-wanted physical body long ago. I pictured the dark, subterrane chamber at Chaythe Asylum, the one where Enid had been subjected to numerous experiments. While under the influence of experimental drugs, the poor girl had likely been subjected to much more...

"So, Dr. Corvine got her pregnant and then the Occupant took hold of Enid... It had her mind, her body and it tried to escape that night, probably to Milsbourne, where it would be able to forge itself a physical body?" I asked.

"No, the goddamn Pope did. Are you deaf or just stupid, professor?" she barked back at me. "Don't mess with anything that doesn't belong to you, and don't go anywhere. I'll be back in a while. Get some sleep. You two look like shit." With that, she was out the door, slamming it behind her and hastily locking it.

Jake and I were left in stunned silence.

4

_____

We weren't thirty minutes into our mandated nap time when Jake looked over at me from the sofa and asked, "We're not really going to kill her, are we?"

I *really* didn't want to talk about it. For starters, the idea of killing Elizabeth Morrissey, no matter what'd taken up residence inside of her, turned my stomach. More than that, I didn't want to be thinking about the Occupant at all—I wanted, *craved*, sleep. His broaching of that difficult subject got my mental machinery running again and a handful of questions started bouncing around what should have been a quiet and empty mind.

"It's too early to worry about that," I said. "We still have to find her, still have to learn more about this town and what the Occupant really is. There could be some other way out, so don't fret."

That wasn't good enough for Jake, who rolled onto his stomach and buried his face in the sofa cushion. "But... but what if she's pregnant?" he asked. "What if... what if she's carrying, like... my kid?"

I stood up, pawing at my burning eyes, and walked into the kitchen to scavenge in the fridge. I zeroed in on an ice cold bottle of Labatt Blue that Jane had likely been saving and, doing the cost-benefit analysis, decided it was worth the risk of pissing her off and popped the top. "If you were worried about that, then you should have wrapped it up," I replied. "But anyway, whatever she's carrying... let's just say it isn't a kid. Not in the traditional sense, anyway. It's a body fit for the Occupant, get it?" I took a glug of beer. The date on the bottle was more than a month passed, but it was still drinkable. "We'll find some way to fix this. We're bringing Elizabeth home with us, come Hell or high water. There's no sense in losing sleep over it, OK?"

Jake nodded, seemed to finally agree, but losing sleep was exactly what he chose to do, rolling onto his back to stare at the ceiling. "Can we trust this lady?" he asked.

"Jane?" I leaned back in the recliner, a splotchy olive green thing, until the leg rest popped out. "We can trust her, yeah. As much as we can trust anyone in the world about this. Why? You know someone else with first-hand experience in the matter?"

He frowned. "It's not that. I mean... the Occupant was in her, once. Right? She still sees it sometimes, is still affected by it. So... do you think that she can actually be trusted, or is the Occupant just using her to manipulate us?"

"You've watched too many horror films," I said. "To my knowledge, she was the first to make real contact with the Occupant, but it couldn't use her to fulfill its goals. She wasn't fertile. And anyhow, the Occupant has certain criteria. It likes a certain kind of host. Enid and Elizabeth both made the grade, so it stands to reason there's something about these Lancaster ladies that gets the monster going." I meditated over a mouthful of beer, continuing the thread of conversation in my head. *But, what?*

Elizabeth and Enid had a last name in common, but were they related by blood? It was too early to say, but I had a feeling it was so.

Jake drifted off after a time, snoring peacefully with his hands behind his head.

Sleep wasn't so kind to me, however. It stood me up.

I finished the beer, got rid of the empty, and then camped out in the chair waiting for the fatigue to overpower me. Instead, I found my gaze wandering about the room, where I began to notice things. The light coming from between the blinds in the living room was thinning. The wind was picking up, and with it came a fresh burst of rain —each drop of which could be heard against the tin roof. There were other sounds, too. The occasional creak I couldn't place; the odd vocal sound—human or animal I couldn't be sure—ringing out from the wilderness just outside.

Jake didn't stir. If his ears picked up anything, he gave no sign of it. Not for the first time, I envied him. I wished that I could shut my eyes and dive into a carefree sleep, cutting away from the inside of this trailer whose scenery seemed to be slowly closing in around me.

The blinds shifted—probably due to a draft—but at their very borders I thought I glanced squinting eyes peering in at me from out in the dusk. The chair made a terrible squeal—a death rattle—as I leaned back further and tried to get comfortable. Something, a spring perhaps, seemed to shift beneath me, to dig into my ass of its own accord, and I couldn't help but picture something inhabiting the small space underneath the chair, preparing to lash out at me from beneath the olive green skirting.

Stop being so paranoid. You need to sleep. For once, you're in a safe place. The thing is in Milsbourne now—it hasn't followed you. Not all the way here. Relax.

No sooner did I train myself to avoid the noises of this unfamiliar place did I begin to feel that I was being watched. The feeling took hold slowly; so slowly that I couldn't be sure I was in its grip until it had closed around me with unendurable tightness. My heart kicked around in my chest like it needed to break out and have a look around the room itself. I clawed at the arm rests of the recliner as though it were a dentist's chair, but I'll be damned if I *saw* anything that should have inspired such a reaction in me. The room was still, silent. A bit darker now that night was setting in, but there was nothing awry.

The hairs on my arms started sticking up, each of them combing through the air like tiny feelers and becoming trained on the threat that my other stupid, unrefined mammalian senses had overlooked. I shut my eyes, but as I did so my ears picked up something like footsteps. Slow, shuffling, but deliberate footsteps. Forcing my eyes open once more, I looked to the window, watched as the blinds were sent rocking by the draft. I caught only my own frightened reflection on the edge of the glass.

The sound of footsteps had ceased. I sucked in a deep breath, let my body uncoil against the recliner. *See? You imagined it.*

Just then, a new noise registered.

The trying of the doorknob.

It rattled in the stillness, the sound capturing my attention at once. I verified it with my sight as well—the copper knob was moving from side to side, throwing off hints of light from the fixture over the kitchen table.

My fear became absolute.

It's here. It's come for us.

Staggering out of the chair as the knob continued its rattling, I dove nearly headfirst into the garbage can and dug out the empty beer bottle I'd tossed away earlier. Clutching it tightly in my hand, I stood beside the door, ready to clock any intruder with it, and held my breath.

"*Jake...*" I whispered. "*It's here.*"

He didn't wake up.

I was going to have to face this on my own.

5

A key slid into the lock and, moments later, Jane came in through the door, eyeing me first with surprise, and then extreme annoyance. Patting the gun I knew to be strapped to her chest, she shook her head. "Put that shit down, you idiot. Why aren't you sleeping? You're losing your damn mind."

I dropped the beer bottle back into the garbage bin with a sheepish smile. "Sorry. I thought I heard something... I just haven't been the same since all of this started."

She shut the door and then proceeded to take off her jacket, getting to business right away while I tried to shake off my embarrassment. "I spoke to a few old-timers in town. None knew of a place called Milsbourne—except for one, Paul Coleman, who seemed to me awfully shifty when I brought it up. I plied him with a couple of beers and asked again when his buddies left the bar, but even then he didn't want to talk. I had to shake him down. He only told me a bit. He says there is a place by that name in the woods—that he knows it because he could supposedly trace his bloodline all the way back to some miners who once lived out that way.

But he went on to say that sensible folk don't have any business going there, and he wouldn't tell me where it was except to give me a real general outline. I already knew it was in the hills, near the old copper mines, and he didn't help me narrow things down at all with his hushed talk." She eyed the empty beer bottle in the trash wistfully, like she wished she'd gotten to it before I had.

"So, that's it, huh?" It was good to know that there were some people in the area who were acquainted with Milsbourne, but I really felt as though we'd taken a few steps back in learning that those same people weren't willing to discuss it. "Seems like getting straight talk on this old town is going to be like sniffing out the real deal on Area 51, huh?"

"So it seems," replied Jane, leaning against the counter and crossing her arms. "Anyhow, we're setting out in the morning. I know the general area. If we're lucky, we'll find it. Lots of ghost towns out there left forgotten in these woods, but you never know."

I agreed, but for one caveat. "Sure, but shouldn't we set out now?" I asked. "Time is in short supply, Jane. My student is out there getting ready to birth some monstrosity into the world and I think that we should—"

"I don't give a damn what you think," she countered, pointing at the recliner. "It's night time. The Occupant has every advantage over us in the dark. Hell, it's got every advantage in the daylight, too, but at least we can see where the fuck we're going during the day. Getting lost in those woods at night is no joke. Plus, your dumb ass needs to get some sleep. Pronto. Make like the boy over there and rest. I won't have you holding me back tomorrow."

"Yeah, fine," I replied. Dropping into the recliner, I stretched out and rested my hands in my lap.

Jane paused between the kitchen and living room and

eyed Jake narrowly. Nodding at him, she asked in a low voice, "Can we trust him?"

"Who, Jake? Yeah, of course we can trust him. He's been mixed up in this with me from the very beginning. And it's his girlfriend we're looking for," I said.

"That's what I'm afraid of." Jane paced through the living room, stopping outside one of the bedrooms and shooting me daggers. "When the time comes, we're going to have to do whatever it takes to stop that thing. You do understand that, right? There's no room for error... no room for *mercy*." Her jaw tensed. "If he gets in the way..."

"I understand. I think he'll be fine," I replied. "He's a good kid. Strong. I think we should explore every option, Jane, but if it comes down to that... he'll make the right choice and not interfere."

Jane chortled. "You want to '*explore every option*', do you? Considering what's at stake here, I think the only option we'll be exploring is the caliber of bullet we'll use in putting her down." She stepped into the bedroom, shutting the door behind her and locking it. "Sleep well."

I sighed, laying into the headrest and staring at the ceiling. *Gee, with a pep talk like that one, how could I possibly not sleep well?*

RAGGED and hungry for sleep though I was, I couldn't drift off for more than a few minutes at a time. I guessed this was what insomniacs had to deal with most nights; sleep would wander close—close enough to grasp—only to flutter off like a butterfly, out of reach.

Resting uneasily in the recliner, listening to Jake's snoring and wishing I could sleep as soundly, noises in and around the trailer kept me awake. The scraping of a branch on the siding, the hooting of an owl in some nearby tree, knocked the heaviness from my eyes and left me on full alert whenever sleep began to feel like a certainty. I yearned for a pair of earplugs, anything to block out the noises of the place. The breeze—hard and bringing with it traces of rain from time to time—made the trailer groan as it settled in the night-time coolness.

As the hours passed and I fidgeted in the chair, other things began to spur my wakefulness. Heavy eyes on the cusp of sleep would begin to fall closed, only to glimpse a dark shape in the corner of the room, near the kitchen. It was like something seen through the lens of a camera, appearing just before the closing of the shutter.

The Occupant.

I noticed it first during a particularly harsh burst of wind that left the trailer rocking and the light over the kitchen sink flickering. Bent and staring from the corner, its shape appearing to mar the wall behind it in a grotesque shadow many times larger than its wiry frame should have allowed, it was gone before I could sit up and cast my sleepless eyes upon it in full. Momentarily awake, my heart crashing in my chest, I stifled a yelp and took a slow pan of the room, finding nothing out of place. Only Jake was there with me, where he looked poised to remain in his coma-like state till morning.

I shut my eyes again, told myself all the usual stories. I blamed my imagination, called it paranoia or a trick of the light, and began courting sleep once more, but with the drooping of my eyelids came another flash of the malign. Crouching in the corner, tangled, orange hair threading out into a wild mane, it cast its ebon eyes on me and loosed a soupy wheeze from its gaping mouth. The shape of its malformed face would have almost looked serpentine in the shadows if not for the enormity of its eyes. One, as big as a saucer, loomed large, as dark as a hole in the earth. The other, smaller, sank unnaturally down its paper-white face like the yolk of a cracked, spoiled egg.

As before, when I jolted fully awake, it was gone.

I covered my eyes with my hands, kneaded them with the heels of my palms, and was prepared to stay in that pathetic pose till morning when a curious noise sounded from above. Raindrops, or perhaps falling acorns, struck the roof, but from where I sat it sounded more like the pitter-patter of feet. A bleary upward glance yielded traces of movement, as of a dark smear, crawling rapidly across the ceiling. The tendrils of dark, orange hair that fanned out in its wake seemed to me the limbs of some exotic species of centipede.

Mashing the pads of my fingers against the armrests, I stared up at the dim ceiling with wide eyes and realized I saw nothing, save for the beige, popcorn texturing.

It's followed us, even here, I thought. *It'll never leave. Not until it's gotten what it wants. Once you've been touched by it, it holds sway over you forever...*

I tried not to whimper, and ignored the sounds that reached my ears in the interim. The vague rustlings outside the window, as of a clumsy, groping animal... The whispers riding in on the wind as of several voices mumbling conspiratorially... The creaks of the exterior as the structure braced against the wind—or else against the hands of unseen visitors in the night.

It wants to get under your skin. It's feeding on your fear... Don't give in. Ignore it. Sleep. You need to sleep! None of this is real... You're safe here...

Sleep and I weren't on speaking terms anymore, though.

I was going to be kept awake till my heart gave out from exhaustion—till my nerves couldn't handle the strain and my brain simply powered off like a television getting its cord pulled out of the wall. Sweat began to form along my brow. My throat tightened. Though my eyes were shut hard, the hairs on my arms and neck perked up in the draft, knocked this way and that as though something had just moved swiftly past.

I don't know how long I remained in this state, quivering, before the exhaustion became too much and I began nodding off once again. I felt my head loll, my breathing slow. Sleep began to cement my eyes shut and I did my best to focus on nothing but the shabby fabric of the chair. My only job was to sink as deeply into the weathered cushions as possible and abandon these surroundings.

I was very nearly there when I felt the cool hand close tightly around my mouth.

I started violently.

Seconds passed. Shaky breaths were taken.

Still, the feeling of that hand did not abate.

This, then, was *real*.

I opened my bloodshot eyes and saw Jane standing to one side of me. It was her hand clasped around my mouth, and she herself was panting, staring straight ahead, through the kitchen, at the door to the trailer.

In her hand was the black handgun.

The words she spoke next were uttered so quietly I almost couldn't hear them over the roar of my pulse. "We've got company," she said, slowly rising to her feet. The gun rose, too, and she fixed its business end upon the door.

6

The doorknob was moving. Someone was trying it furtively from the outside. It shifted to the right, then to the left, the mechanisms within giving off a faint rattle. The deadbolt had been thrown and the door didn't budge, but as the moments passed the would-be intruder began to force the door more overtly. The hinges quaked as hands were pressed against the exterior.

"I know you're out there," called Jane. Her voice boomed throughout the quiet trailer. It was this that finally woke Jake. The kid's eyes flashed open and in his surprise he fell off of the couch, burying one knee in the carpet and dizzily gaining his feet. With her finger resting on the trigger of that mean-looking piece, she side-stepped towards the door and placed a hand against the deadbolt. "Who is it?"

Someone feeble-voiced stammered from the other side of the door. "It's m-me, Jane. It's Paul. Me and some guys from town... just wanna talk."

Jane had mentioned a Paul earlier that evening—Paul had been the evasive one in town, the one who'd known a thing or two about Milsbourne, but who hadn't been willing to tell her much. What he was doing trying to break into the trailer late at night—and why he'd brought with him 'some guys from town'—remained to be seen, but I hardly imagined they'd come all this way just to chat.

Without a word, Jane unlocked the deadbolt, threw the door aside with her foot and gave the visitors outside a good look at the gun in her fist.

From the chair in the living room I couldn't be altogether sure, but there looked to be roughly five or six men waiting outside the trailer.

And most of them had guns of their own.

Jake and I froze. One minute we'd been sleeping peacefully—or trying to sleep, in my case—and the next we'd been transported back to the O.K. Corral. The men outside the door were a slovenly bunch. All were dressed in ragged clothes—flannel, jeans, overalls—and had their rifles at the ready. A backwoods firing squad. Those who didn't have guns were carrying what looked to be either thick tree branches or pieces of rebar; I couldn't tell which from the seat I was plastered to.

Jane didn't flinch, like being held up by an angry mob was an everyday thing for her. She kept the gun pointed at the mass of visitors ahead and looked ready to squeeze the trigger at the slightest provocation. Had the wind blown just the right way, she might've taken a few of their heads off without the least hesitation. "Got ourselves a standoff, I see." She licked her lips. "Now, I'd hate to send you back to your wives and daughters in coffins, so I'll ask you plainly..." She looked to the man at the front of the pack, unarmed, which I took to be Paul Coleman. "What've you brought this ugly bunch to my doorstep for, Paul?"

Paul, a thin and sweaty man whose teeth were mostly missing and whose depleted hairline gave way to a sheaf of wispy, shoulder-length hair, looked real apologetic—though the gun in his face might have been the reason for that. He kneaded his hands at his waist and looked to Jane with sorrowful eyes. "Jane, I'm sorry. I... I wasn't t-tryin' to bother ya. You see, I was hopin' we could t-talk..."

"What about?" interrupted Jane. "I take it this is the conversation you *didn't* want to have back at the bar? Why you feeling so talkative all of a sudden?"

Before Paul could blather on, someone else in the group, a tall and solid man with a red, sweat-stained T-shirt and a shotgun in his beefy hands, spoke up. "I asked Paul here to introduce me to the woman who was asking him all those questions about that place in the woods." He took a step forward, the gun lowered to his side. Jane shifted her aim so that a bullet from her piece would have sailed clean through his heart, but he seemed unbothered. "It's just that, when people ask questions about that place out in the woods, I can't help but get a little... *overprotective*, I guess you might say."

"And why's that?" asked Jane, not missing a beat.

"Because there are things in those woods that ain't none of your business," replied the tall man.

Jane wasn't the kind of woman you talked down to, and it was probably just the fact that she was outnumbered that kept her from blowing his brains out and shutting him up for good. "Who the hell do you think you are?" she asked.

The man took another step forward, and Paul, standing beside him, flinched in anticipation of a gunshot that, thankfully, didn't come. "As a matter of fact, I'm Eli Lancaster, and I'm going to say it again—those woods ain't none of your business. You'd do well to stay out of 'em. And if you can't, I'd be happy to help you stay out of 'em by putting your ass down right here and now."

Things had reached a boiling point. Someone was going to pull a trigger or take a swing any second now.

I piped up from the living room and managed to ease the tension by a fraction when I asked, "Wait, your name is *Lancaster?*"

The man and all of his goons looked past Jane confusedly. "Who the hell is he?" asked Eli before clearing his throat and answering, more loudly, "It is. What about it?"

Jane was about to protest when I stood up and waved the man inside. "Let him in. We need to talk." Jane's anger boiled over and for a moment I expected her to turn the gun on me. "Let him in. He may have the information we're looking for." I glanced at Eli, arching a brow. "Care to talk? I think we may be able to help each other out."

Jane fumed as Eli stepped past her. He nodded to his band of grungy companions and stationed himself in the kitchen, shrugging. "So, who are you?"

"He's a rude good-for-nothing who's wearing out his welcome—" began Jane before I managed to cut her off.

"Who I am isn't important. Suffice it to say, you and I are probably on the same side." I approached him, tried to shake his hand, but he wouldn't accept it. Undeterred, I pressed him once more. "What's going on in the woods? Tell me everything you know."

7

To my relief, tensions thawed just enough for a conversation to take place. Eli lowered his firearm. Jane did the same. He pointed at me with a thick, stubby finger, the nail clotted with dirt. I wasn't sure what this guy did for a living, but I'd have bet he worked outdoors. "What do *you* know about all of this?" He looked me up and down, confusion and perhaps incredulity marring his rugged features as he did so. "You don't look like you're from around here."

"I'm not," I replied. "I'm a college professor, from Ohio. But that's not what we need to talk about." I buried my hands in my pockets and looked to him earnestly. "The thing in the woods. I've seen it with my own two eyes." Nodding towards Jake, I added, "It's hitched a ride in a friend of ours and it led us all the way here, to Michigan."

Whatever calm may have existed within Eli's expression slowly faded away as he donned a sour frown. He looked down at the ground, giving a shake of his head, and then looked back to Jane.

"It's true," she said. "He isn't lying."

Wiping at his nose, Eli Lancaster adjusted his overalls. "Tell you the truth, I don't think you understand what it is you're poking around in. I don't know what you saw—what *led* you lot out here—but I recommend you get back to Ohio. It'll be safer for everyone involved. What's going on in these woods is no one's business but mine." His jaw tensed, frame became rigid. "Do I make myself clear?"

Oh, he'd made himself clear, all right. He didn't want to tell us what he knew of the Occupant. Maybe he thought we'd get in his way, or else he had some other reason to keep us in the dark. Whatever the case, I was getting annoyed with his replies. If not for the gun in his hand, I might've been pushier.

Instead, I had to play the diplomat. "Listen, I'm not trying to give you a hard time. We're outsiders, and I know that we must seem like a real nuisance, but this is a life or death situation. Something—which seems to have a strong connection to these woods, and to the ghost town of Milsbourne—has taken hold of a friend. She's disappeared, into the forest. We need your help if we're going to have any chance of rescuing her."

Eli twitched at the mention of Milsbourne, but sympathy seemed to be lacking completely in his expression. He shook his head, took in a deep breath. His grip on the gun tightened. "I'm telling you, you don't know the half of it. Go back to where y'all came from, all of you. It ain't no business of yours. I'm sorry to hear that your friend's been having some issues. If she's lost in the woods, maybe she'll find her way to a road or something."

Jane looked incensed, and stepped up to challenge him. Standing beside Eli, looking up at him with a steely gaze, she crossed her arms. "We know what's hiding in those woods."

Eli tongued his molars. "I rather doubt it."

Years ago, Jane herself had been possessed by the Occupant. Her uncle had subjected her to hideous experiments in a cabin within these very woods. To be so easily dismissed by Eli sent her into a rage that she could barely contain.

I spoke up before she gave into the impulse to shoot him. "We just want to know what you know, all right? Why has this thing come all the way back to Milsbourne? How did you first become acquainted with it?"

"It's my family's business," he replied curtly. "It's the curse of my family line, and I'm not about to give a bunch of outsiders a detailed history. I thought I made it clear to you that it's none of your business—it's mine, and mine alone. I don't know what mischief your friend has gotten up to, but let's just say that, if she's really walked into the heart of these woods, then she ain't coming back out. My family left Milsbourne behind with all the others, moved away from it, because of what lurked there. There's no reason why you— or even *you*," he said, motioning to Jane, "should know about it. You leave the woods alone and you might just enjoy a long life. I assume you're smart enough to follow simple directions, ain't ya, *professor*? Now and then we get people poking around—think they know something about Milsbourne, about its history—"

"People like Jamieson Monroe?" I chanced.

Eli's eyes narrowed—possibly in recognition—but he didn't pick up that thread.

"I don't know why you're being so secretive," I said. "There's something out there, and it's—"

It was his turn to interrupt me, and he did so with a not-so-subtle shifting of the gun in his hand. "If there *is* something happening in these woods, then I'll take care of it.

Don't you worry about what's out there." He looked to me, then to Jake. Turning towards the door, he paused only long enough to tell Jane, "I'ma tell you one last time. Stay out of the woods. If I find you there, poking around where you ain't supposed to, it's very possible I'm going to have a hunting accident." He paced through the kitchen, out the door, and gave a little bob of his head as he exited the trailer. "Y'all have a good night, now."

Jane was seething. I waited for her to unload her magazine into the throng of men outside, but they walked off, muttering, and she simply remained in the living room, quaking in anger.

Jake cleared his throat, breaking the taut silence. "So, what're we gonna do? Are we going to have to stand down, then?"

"Not a chance in hell," spat Jane. "I don't know who he thinks he is, and I don't care. We're going in there after the Occupant and there ain't shit he can do about it." She holstered her gun and strode to the door, slamming it shut and locking it.

"He knows something," I said, leaning against the wall. I peered through the window from between a crack in the blinds. The mass of roughs had walked far from the trailer now, could scarcely be seen as they meandered into the distance. "He said it was the 'curse' of his family line. Just what was *that* supposed to mean?"

Jane was too enraged to answer, but Jake spoke up with a half-formed guess before trailing off. "Well, if this has to do with the Lancaster family line—and Elizabeth is supposedly descended from that line—then..."

The surname "Lancaster" had been popping up an awful lot lately, like a crafty, grinning toy peeking out of the holes in a Whac-A-Mole cabinet. One of these days I was going to crack it in the skull and win the game, but not today. *Enid Lancaster* had been the Occupant's most famous host to date. Dale and Louisa Morrissey had shared with us the scarce details of Elizabeth's true parentage—she'd been born of a mother by the name of *Ophelia Lancaster*, and her probable birth location had been in the vicinity of unincorporated Milsbourne. Now we had this Eli Lancaster fellow, who was mighty secretive about the Occupant, and who wanted us to stay out of the woods so badly that he'd come by with his posse in the middle of the night to intimidate us.

What was Eli's game? Was he on the Occupant's side, seeking to protect it? It seemed like a real possibility. Why else would he be so secretive? For that matter, how did his family line figure into all of this—why did the Occupant have such a strong taste for the women of the Lancaster lineage?

If Eli Lancaster wasn't going to talk—and I felt sure he wasn't—then we had nowhere else to look for answers but in old Milsbourne itself. It wasn't likely that a worm-eaten, abandoned mining town in the middle of the woods would yield much in the way of clues, however Eli's insistence that we stay away inspired in me a minor hope that we'd find some lead worth following there.

"Get some sleep," ordered Jane, marching back to her room. "We're setting out in the morning. Early."

Jake and I didn't feel much like sleeping just then— believe me, nothing wakes you up like having a gun shoved in your face—but somehow, a few minutes after dimming the lights, we were both able to drift off. I extended the leg rest and fell asleep with my hands in my lap, open-mouthed. Snoring till an hour past dawn, I awoke to a parched tongue, sore throat, and to Jane's cutting gaze. The look in her eyes was every bit as intense as it'd been the night before—rather than sleep, it seemed to me she'd stayed up all night stoking the flames of her anger.

She tossed a foil-wrapped pair of toaster pastries at me and Jake and then started pouring fresh coffee into mugs. "Get your asses up. Got work to do."

8

J ane devised the day's itinerary over Pop-Tarts and strong coffee.

She stuffed bags full of the gear she had on hand and explained that we'd have to make a pitstop at a general store some twenty miles away for a few other items. Among the things she'd already owned were knives, backpacks, guns, ammunition, jugs of purified water and boxes of edibles such as protein bars and beef jerky. There was also a large tent—big enough, she insisted, to fit all three of us comfortably.

Hauling these bags into the bed of her truck, Jane returned to the kitchen table and slurped up a mouthful of coffee as she drew an invisible map across the table with her finger. I didn't know what landmarks she was describing but it was clear she was able to picture it all very clearly in her mind. "I know a route into the woods that should keep us pretty well-hidden most of the way." She tapped one corner of the table and began to trace a more or less straight line some distance in. "It'll be a half-day march till we get to the mines, and even then, we may have to go farther still in order to hit the right town. I don't know that I've ever been to Milsbourne, so we'll have to keep our eyes peeled for any useful landmarks." She drew a circle with her fingertip at the table's center. "Now, once we get there, we're going to establish a camp. We'll find some dry land, preferably up on the hills where we'll have a good vantage point. That'll help us keep an eye out for Eli and his thugs—or anything else we might encounter in the woods."

The way she said that last part, I knew she wasn't much concerned about bears or wolves.

She continued. "I don't know what Eli is going to be doing in the woods, if he's gone there at all. If he has, then it's possible he and his goons will get the jump on the Occupant. Maybe they'll put her down and save us the trouble." Ignoring Jake's protestations, she lectured on. "Otherwise, maybe we'll luck out and the ol' girl will cut down all of those bastards, tiring herself out. I wouldn't mind an easy target."

I was confident that Jane knew the woods and that she'd be able to get us where we needed to go. What I feared, though, was what we'd actually do once we got there. For starters, I'd been briefly lost in the woods at night, and knew how easy it was to fall sway to a paralyzing terror. Once we set foot within that forest, we were on the Occupant's turf— would be as helpless as we'd been while wandering blind in Chaythe Asylum.

Then there was the threat posed by Eli. I had no doubt that he'd make good on his promise to gun us down if we crossed paths in the woods. What his motivations were— whether he was aligned with the Occupant or against it—I couldn't be sure, but that he and his men represented a potent danger was a given. The absolute worst thing I could think of would be to wander into the woods in the hopes of saving Elizabeth only to get gunned down by one of those assholes. Talk about anti-climactic.

It was decided that Jake would be our pack mule, and the bulk of the supplies were packed onto his back for a quick test run. He managed to carry his load without complaint, though whether his muscular frame would be able to manage a half-day's hike under such weigh remained to be seen. Jane talked up his strength, made fun of me for being comparatively puny, though in her assigning him the role of mule, I suspected she had an ulterior motive.

It'd been clear for some time that Jane and Jake didn't see eye to eye on the matter of how to deal with Elizabeth. For her part, Jane probably thought it best to weigh Jake down, to handicap him, so that—in the event of an encounter with the thing—she'd be able to outrun him and take down the Occupant without opposition.

Jake wanted to save his girlfriend, to find some way to exorcise the Occupant so that we could bring Elizabeth home with us. Jane, on the other hand, wanted to kill her, and wouldn't hesitate to pull the trigger if the opportunity presented itself. I saw the reason behind both stances but, forced to choose right then and there, would not have been able to put myself in either camp. Elizabeth was a student of mine, and I felt responsible, at least partially, for this mess she was now in. Still, allowing her to live—and allowing the Occupant to use her body—would result in horrors hitherto only whispered of.

For the hundredth time—or maybe the thousandth—I tried not to think of that inevitable decision and instead focused on the plan Jane was hatching. When she'd mapped out the route in her head, estimated our general time of arrival in the proximity of what she expected would be Milsbourne, she led us out to the truck. Our next stop was the general store.

We rode on in silence. I thought to switch on the radio—to turn on a news program to figure out what was going on in the world, at least—but Jane batted my hand away from the dial and we sat quietly instead. When we finally arrived at the general store, which reminded me of some antiquated trading post straight out of a western movie, Jane hesitated before letting us out of the truck. "Come on," she said after a brief pause. "I'll need help carrying stuff."

The squat building lacked air conditioning. That wouldn't have been a problem for me, except that I'd gotten a nice dose of the spring warmth on the ride in and felt like I was overheating. Three big windows spanned the front wall of the place, and on the other side of them I spied a long counter, atop which was perched a single cash register. It was a black, metallic thing—nothing digital about it. Standing at the counter was a rough-looking bearded man. He was leafing through a newspaper and glanced up at us only briefly as we stepped inside. A ragged length of yarn with a pair of rusted bells on one end was tied to the inside of the door, and they jingled discordantly as we shuffled in.

This "general store" had a little bit of everything on its dusty, sagging shelves. There were tinned foods, basic camping supplies, a limited selection of fishing rods and lures, a large, humming cooler packed with tubs of bait worms, bottles of cheap beer well past their sell-by dates and other junk. It wasn't exactly a Whole Foods.

Jane led us towards the back, our shoes squeaking against the dirty, bubbling linoleum, and to a section stocked with miscellaneous electronic goods. She scooped up a few packs of Duracells to keep our flashlights going. In the meantime, I perused the other stuff on offer. There was a lone boombox—big, black and rectangular—gathering dust on the uppermost shelf. The model on the front of the sun-bleached box looked sort of like Vanilla Ice in his prime, and the boombox itself was probably at least as old. There were a few newer items to be found—handheld radios, charging cables for cell phones long out of production. On the next shelf over were several boxes of Topps baseball cards—dated to 1997—and a Scottie Pippen action figure, posed mid-dunk.

I was about to delve into the next shelf, burdened with Petoskey stones and cheap plastic beach toys, when Jane thrust a handful of items into my hand. "What's this stuff for?" I asked. She'd handed me a few bottles with faded labels, a pack of what looked to be band-aids, and more.

"A makeshift first-aid kit," she said. "Bandages, pain killers. Some bottles of rubbing alcohol, iodine. Gauze, tape. You'll be carrying this stuff."

"The team medic. I like it." I followed her to the next aisle, where she sized up a few boxes of cereal and tins of tuna. Either the contents were as worn out as the containers, or else Jane decided the food she'd packed was good enough, because she decided not to buy any. She led us to the register, taking a couple of bills from a billfold and handing them to the bearded man behind the counter, who looked at the junk in my hands and did some mental math. When he'd finished calculating the cost of our purchases, he leaned on the register, hit some button on it three or four times, and opened the drawer to fish out some change. Handing Jane a few small bills and nickels, he shut the drawer with his hip and we left. Not a word had been exchanged—no "have a nice day" or anything of the kind.

We were back out in the sunlight, walking to the truck. "Think this place is on Yelp?" I asked Jake.

He grinned.

Jane took a few moments packing all of the new acquisitions into our bags and then threw open the passenger side door, waving us in. "Let's get to it," she said.

We both knew what that meant. I couldn't help but drag my feet as I approached the truck. *Great. It's time to re-enter those dark woods again.*

It was a lovely day for a hike, and under any other circumstances I might've been jazzed about spending the day outdoors. Though the sunlight was a little too warm for my likes, the breeze was pleasant and the skies were clear. I put on my seatbelt as I sat between Jake and our grim-faced driver, and reminded myself of what we'd be faced with when the sun set some hours from now.

I looked to the roadside, to the clustered trees that popped up in virtually every direction. Where there was no road or building, there were trees.

And in between those trees, very soon, would grow a maddening darkness.

The truck started onto the main road, weaving a bit as Jane pulled open a bottle of water and took a deep drink.

"How far are we? From this path you're talking about?" I asked.

Jane answered without missing a beat, like she'd been doing the arithmetic in her head at that very moment. "Forty minutes. It's a little roundabout, but it should get us to where we're going."

A part of me wished the starting point for our hike was closer; forty minutes was a lot of time to sit and think about all of the things that could go wrong.

Jake was on a similar wave-length, hands sandwiched between his knees and gaze pasted to the green, fluttering scenery outside the window. There wasn't enough room for all of us to exist comfortably in the cabin of the truck, but to his credit, he didn't complain about being cooped up against me. Stretching his long legs as best he could, he sighed and asked no one in particular, "Do you think she's OK?"

"I'm sure Elizabeth's fine," was my reply, delivered so fast I wasn't even sure I bought it myself.

Jane chortled. "*Fine?* I doubt it."

Jake and I looked to her—he with alarm, I with annoyance.

"What do you think she's going through?" asked Jake. "You were possessed by the Occupant once, right? But now you're OK. What was it like, back then?"

Jane scratched at her scalp like she was fixing to uproot her blonde locks, evidently bothered by the question—or the remembrance—but she quickly composed herself and placed both hands on the wheel. "It's, uh... It was different in my case," she said, giving Jake a sidelong glance. "It didn't want me. Not the way it wanted Enid, or your girlie. I wasn't a good fit. But it did take up residence for a little while. Off and on." She tapped her forehead. "While it was in there, it was unlike anything I've ever experienced. Imagine being smothered inside your own body." She shuddered, taking a pack of cigarettes from her pocket but then putting them back. "What she's going through must be loads worse, though."

"Why's that?" asked Jake.

"Because it wants her for keeps."

Jane's words hung in the air for some time. I tried to think of something I could say to ease Jake's worry, but came up empty-handed. Nothing was going to help this shit sandwich go down.

"What happens if..." Jake trailed off, but Jane knew more or less where he was going.

"If the Occupant uses her to make itself a new body? I don't know, but I have a guess. Whatever happens, I don't imagine it's going to be good for the host, you know?" She shook her head, eased into a right turn. "A thing like that will probably kill its host. I'm not even sure it'll be a pregnancy in the usual sense—could take nine months, could take less. But even if she somehow survived all of this, your girlfriend isn't going to be the same person. Once that thing has been inside of you, it ruins you. Believe me, I know first-hand. I've been through a lot of shit in my life, but till my dying day I'll never be able to fully put the Occupant behind me."

"Elizabeth is a fighter," said Jake. His voice wavered like he didn't really buy it, so he said it a second time, more forcefully. "She's a fighter. I think she'll pull through. We just need to get to her and maybe try an exorcism."

"An exorcism?" I fought back the urge to laugh. "I'll give Father Merrin a call."

Jane simply shook her head. "There's no exorcising the Occupant, kid. The Occupant, in some small way, exists in all of us. It's in that dark space—the one in the corner of your eye—always looking out. It doesn't sleep. The only thing we can do—and the only thing the girl would want us to do—is put her down."

Whether Jake had finally made peace with this, or whether he was deep in thought, searching for some as yet unnamed alternative, I couldn't be sure.

Meanwhile, the foliage flanking both sides of the road was getting thicker.

9

W e arrived at our destination.

Getting there involved a bit of off-roading. Jane took the pickup down a dirt path that wound some miles off of a main road, and then into a narrow corridor of overgrown grass, at the end of which was something like a dirt parking lot. The recent rain had left this patch of ground rather wet, and the dense tree cover had kept the bulk of the moisture in place, resulting in a thick layer of shoe-grasping mud.

She threw the truck into park and nodded at the scene through the windshield. "This will take us to where we want to go. A good eight or nine hours north and we'll hit the edge of the mines. Could be a little farther than that before we hit Milsbourne; I've only gone up this way once or twice, and never to look specifically for a town."

Jake and I stepped out, stretching our legs. I leaned against the side of the vehicle, worked my knees and shoulders till they cracked. Draping a backpack over one shoulder and a loosely-packed duffel full of medical supplies across my chest, I took a deep breath. The stuff didn't feel too heavy and I imagined it wouldn't slow me down.

The way ahead was curiously dark, the thick foliage swaying in the breeze but admitting very little sunlight. The path ahead was one of perpetual dusk. It was a stretch to call this area "virginal", and yet as I scanned our surroundings, the three of us and the dirty truck we'd brought were the only aberrations. There wasn't a candy wrapper, a soda bottle to be seen. The trees, their roots threading the ground like fat veins, looked as though they'd been undisturbed for ages, and in the shadow their limbs bobbed up and down, almost as though they were taking turns peering down at us.

I didn't have long to marvel at our surroundings. The gravity of our mission intruded, and within minutes we were walking into the woods. Jane had a bag strapped to her back and a rifle in her hand. Before leaving the truck, she gave me her handgun—helped me strap it to my chest despite my complete lack of experience with firearms. Jane insisted that more than one of us needed armed, and she gave me a crash course in how to use it, even though the thought left me somewhat nervous.

"The safety's off. You only point it at something you want to kill. Squeeze the trigger, don't pull it. There's a good bit of recoil, too, so be prepared for that. It comes out of the holster real smooth—make sure to get used to its weight in your hand." She tightened the holster around my shoulder and made me hold the gun till I had the grip right. "And always keep a round in the chamber," she added, racking the slide.

I'd never fired a gun in my life and was more than a little uneasy with such a massive piece strapped to my chest. If push came to shove, I wasn't sure I'd be able to use it with any proficiency. Frankly, I expected to be more a liability with it than anything. At more than one junction, Jake offered to carry the handgun instead. He'd done some work with his dad at the firing range and knew the basics. Jane absolutely refused to let him handle it, though, and I knew why.

She didn't want him getting in the way. If she let him hold onto the gun, there was every chance Jake would turn it on her when the time for action finally came—rather than on our target.

Feeling like Rambo, I straightened the straps on my back pack to keep from brushing against the holster and fell into step behind Jane.

The ground was soupy in places; there were patches of overgrown grass, of dirt, gravel, but everywhere we stepped the recent rains made for soft, damp terrain. Clustered around the bases of trees, I spied large, pale mushrooms whose mist-covered lobes bloomed chaotically. Moss stained many of the trees in layers so thick they must have been decades in the making. A number of birds bobbed and weaved about the treetops, but were reduced to black, winged smears by the oppressive shadow.

I couldn't help but be unnerved by this wilderness. Perhaps during the day, and so far from our final destination, we were reasonably safe. Though things were dark, we'd be able to see most approaching threats and prepare ourselves against an attack.

That wouldn't be the case after dark.

Perhaps it was the fresh air that loosened him up, however Jake proved rather talkative. He regaled the two of us with brief stories about his childhood. "My dad and I never got along too well. He's a hard-ass, real strict. But now and then, in the summers when he could get the time off work, he'd take me out to the woods—to some place real

scenic down south—and we'd go camping for a week or two.
I loved it. It was the only time my dad and I were ever, like...
close. He taught me how to build a fire, how to fish and hunt.
It's the only time of my life, except for holidays, when I can
remember him being genuinely happy and carefree."

I wasn't sure why he was telling us this; I guessed that
the earthiness in the breeze had roused some latent olfac-
tory memory in him. He was soon asking Jane about the
fishing in the area, about the history of the place, and she
gave him clipped answers.

"This land—some of it is what you might call 'virginal'
forest. Untouched by loggers, for the most part. Some
sections got hacked down way back in the day—by miners
and such. But when this area thinned out population-wise,
and certain parts came under government protection, well,
it was left to sit undisturbed. People hike through this area
now and then, but you'll find most outdoorsy types stick to
the established routes. They don't do the kind of off-road
exploration we're doing now. It's not safe, and there are no
guidebooks to keep them from getting lost. It's denser here,
too, which plays tricks on your technology." Jane sighed.
"Some of us locals, though, we get around.

"I remember, after my parents passed away and I came
under my uncle's care, I spent a long time hiking these
woods. It was before things went all crazy—before he got
real serious about his experiments. I'd walk for hours,
finding little bits of old homes, old settlements, and I'd sit in
the shade wondering what kind of people had once lived in
'em, where they'd gone to, what the places had looked like in
their prime. It was my favorite thing to do, and with a
compass I was able to more or less find my way. My uncle
would even come with me now and then. There was a time,
believe it or not, when he was a reasonably caring man."

That was something I *couldn't* believe, but I nodded anyhow. "Hard to picture a guy like W. R. Corvine as a naturalist," I said. "So, that cabin was meant to be his personal Walden, I guess?"

Both Jake and Jane looked to me blankly.

OK, so neither of them were fans of Thoreau.

We wandered on. Jane had a compass in hand—a decidedly old school choice of navigational instrument—and kept us going north. Now and then I looked down at the gun strapped to my chest, my pulse quickening at the thought of it accidentally discharging. Jane noticed and called me out on it. "It'll only fire if you pull the trigger. Newer guns won't even discharge if you drop them out of a helicopter. Only the trigger will do it. Quit stressing."

That was supposed to comfort me, I guess, but it didn't. I felt like I had a time bomb pressing into my breast.

Something in the scenery pulled me out of my own head and made me pause. I stood against a tree trunk, clearing my throat and directing the attention of my companions to my left. Some thirty feet away—or perhaps more, as distance was difficult for me to judge within the tangled forest—I saw what looked to be a human silhouette. My hand rose to touch the handgun, and behind it I could feel the charging of my heart. "There's... there's someone there," I muttered.

The other two said nothing, but froze as they followed my gaze into the woods. Eventually, they singled out the form that'd caught my eye, a leaning thing half-masked by a veil of swaying green. Its shape was that of a leering humanoid figure, and yet the longer I stared, not sensing any movement on its part, the more certain I became that I was looking at some kind of bent, leafless trunk.

Jane sighed deeply and slapped me in the arm. "It's nothing. Just an old tree."

Though he didn't seem quite so sure, Jake stared at the formation a short while and then continued following Jane in silence, keeping his eyes pasted to the forest floor, lest he see something similarly anthropomorphic in the distance.

My heart never did quite slow, because even after the shock faded from my system I found I had to march in double-quick time to keep up with Jane. My pack-a-day habit was catching up to me. I shifted the load on my back and jogged ahead so that I was beside Jake, and started chatting to keep my mind from singling out strange shapes in the wilderness. "What do you think our odds are of encountering Eli and his boys out here?"

Jane looked down at her compass and then stuffed it into her pocket, tossing her shoulders. "Dunno, but if I had to guess, I'd say they're low. They likely set off into the woods last night, looking for the Occupant. If they found her... then I expect things went one of two ways..."

"The Occupant either got them or they managed to put her down," I said, knowing full well that the former scenario was most likely in this case.

Jake stumbled a little, turning his wide eyes to meet mine. "Y-You don't think they hurt her, do you?"

"Based on personal experience, I'm a little more concerned about what she may have done to *them*," I said.

This wasn't good enough for him. He staggered on a few steps, muttering to himself. "I hope they didn't hurt her." He was in another world—a world in which we weren't hunting for a bonafide monster. He was still under the impression that we could somehow sweet-talk the Occupant into giving up its nefarious goals. I wasn't so sure, but I knew one thing: I was damn tired of talking about it. When the time came, we'd have to do something to stop the thing, and I knew that killing the girl wasn't off the table.

"Me too," replied Jane, wetting her lips. "I hope they didn't hurt her." She paused, a slow smile crossing her lips. "I'd like for that to be *my* honor."

10

I wasn't sure how long we'd been walking when we stopped for a smoke break.

With a lit Marlboro in hand, I took a swig from a water jug and squatted onto the trunk of a fallen tree as though it were a bench. My brow had begun accumulating beads of sweat, and as I puffed away they began trickling down my face, making my eyes sting. Somewhere in the last hour or so the temperature had started going up, and despite the lack of direct sunlight I discovered a most inconvenient feature of this dense woodland—the heat, once it broke through the canopy, was trapped. Owing to the recent rains, we were now wading through not only warmth, but humidity.

I pulled the collar of my damp shirt away from my neckline, cursing, and tried to savor the last of my cigarette. Jane joined me on the tree trunk, setting her bag down and crossing her legs. Not bothering to de-load, Jake paced between a pair of white cedars and, when he wasn't smashing granola bars, guzzled spring water. Leaning against one of the trees and choking down the last of his third or fourth Nature Valley bar, he eyed Jane and I curiously.

"What?" I asked him, ashing my cigarette.

"Why do you guys smoke?" he asked. "It's gonna kill you. And it smells like crap."

I blew a puff of smoke in his direction, then glanced down at the burning tip. "Nothing like a good smoke to put hair on your chest," I replied. "Everyone's a critic these days, but when I was a kid, in the 90's, nothing was cooler." I arched a brow. "Nowadays, people like to vape. They have these big, obnoxious-looking contraptions that spew clouds of vapor everywhere. Me? I'll take the elegance and simplicity of a good cigarette any day." I was mostly bullshitting with him, and figured that, if I survived this mess, I'd go shopping for some Nicorette once I got back home.

Looking up at him with an arched brow, Jane had a different answer. "Sure, it might kill me," she said. "But sometimes, just being alive can be Hell. We all need a crutch of some kind to make it through the day, to take the edge off." She took a long drag, then put the cigarette out on the heel of her boot. Her eyes became distant for a moment, and she slumped on the makeshift seat, kneading her hands.

It was easy to forget that Jane had been Dr. Corvine's first subject—the first person, to my knowledge, that'd ever made contact with the Occupant. Her innocence had been stolen by that man, and the bulk of her life had been spent in unceasing terror due to her forced participation in his outre psychological experiments. She hadn't been of the right stock to serve as a portal for the entity—Enid Lancaster would go on to fulfill that role some years later—but the impression that the Occupant had left on her was clear and undeniable. Even though the experiments had taken place more than thirty years ago, Jane had never stopped living in those days, had never been able to fully put those events behind her and resume a normal life. In that sense, it made her assistance on this journey all the more impressive. She was coming with us into the forest, preparing to square off against an evil that'd haunted her for years.

I wasn't quite ready to get moving yet. I took some time stretching my legs, working my ankles in my hands very slowly until they popped. "If you don't mind me asking, what'd you do after your uncle was out of the picture?" I asked her.

She stood, brushing herself off and staring up into the canopy, her face glowing in a narrow shaft of sunlight. "I put the old man in the ground and then I tried to live a normal life," she began. "Of course, there isn't any moving on after that. But I didn't know any better, and I did what I could to live like everyone else. I got a job in town—a few, actually. I spent some time camping out of an old tent, eating canned food, until I could afford to rent my own place. It took awhile, but I eventually bought that trailer, and I've lived in it for a long time now.

"Eventually I got a better job, got involved with a man some years older than me, Rick. It didn't work out, of course. We lived together in that little trailer, but he insisted on drinking himself to death. It wasn't much of a relationship, anyhow. We had fun together, but it wasn't really 'love'. I couldn't open up to him, couldn't tell him the truth about where I'd come from, what I'd experienced. He wouldn't have believed me even if I had. And hell, that ain't the kind of thing you talk about out loud. For a long time, I did my best to bury it. To forget." She shuddered even as she wiped sweat from her forehead. "But I can't forget, and that's why I'm here. You know, I envied Rick. He died ignorant; died without knowing what awaited him after that final curtain. Me, though? I've known for a long time what I'm in for in the end. We're all damned, set to become strands in that black web. I've seen the other side, and when it's time for me to go, you can be sure I'll go kicking and screaming."

I didn't say anything. Nothing out of my mouth would serve to comfort her or change her mind. Instead, I took another gulp of water and held it in my mouth for a beat, taking in the sound of leaves rustling in the wind.

"I don't get it," replied Jake. He seemed awfully bothered by Jane's reply, and fidgeted continuously with the straps of his bags between the pair of towering cedars. "Don't you believe in Heaven?"

Jane shook her head slowly, deliberately, her face marred by evident sadness. "I don't know if there is a Heaven or not, to tell you the truth." She glared back at him, pulling her compass out of her pocket. "What I *do* know is that I wouldn't be welcome there. When a thing like the Occupant has touched your life... when it's been in your head, known your heart... it leaves you changed. Damaged." She looked at the compass, waited until she had a good read, and then started off into the woods, leaving us to clamber after her.

I couldn't help but feel unsettled by her little talk. Though I'd never been strapped to a chair and been used as a puppet by a dark spirit, I'd been touched by the Occupant in my own way. And so had Elizabeth. Jake, too, by extension. Our little group had wandered far closer to this hideous and enigmatic thing than any living person was ever meant to do. If Jane was right, and the fate of those who encountered the Occupant was really that grim...

Let's just say that I felt one hell of an existential crisis coming on.

~

WE'D BEEN MARCHING for hours. Though we'd taken a few breaks along the way, the steady hike through the woods—which, if you can believe it, only seemed to grow *denser* the further we went—had left me feeling beat down.

We were in a secluded pocket now where the trees grew so close together you couldn't get anywhere without taking greenery to the face. Branches had raked our arms and legs along the way, and we were now fairly drenched in a well-earned sweat. The day's heat, filtered through the canopy and converting the puddles into vapor, turned the woods into a goddamn sauna. The visibility in this area, as can be imagined, wasn't so good. If there were any threats looming beyond the next tree, you weren't going to know about them until it was too late.

The problem of the day's heat was set to resolve itself very soon, as the shards of sunlight reaching us from above took on the dull, golden hues of dusk.

"It's going to be getting dark soon," said Jane, funneling some trail mix into her mouth and crunching contemplatively. Her blonde hair was sticking to her forehead and her cheeks were red. The three of us had already run through a jug of water combined, had guzzled it like it was going out of style. We'd brought quite a lot of it with us—the bulk of it hitching a ride on Jake's back—but I wondered for a moment what we'd do if we ran out. Were there bodies of water around here clean enough for us to drink out of? Jane derailed my train of thought as she continued. "We need to start thinking about camp."

I slowly surveyed our surroundings, wondering in which direction the shadowed town of Milsbourne might be found. Up to this point, we'd found nothing in the way of human settlements—historical or contemporary. Having walked for miles and miles we hadn't seen so much as a stray soda can mixed in with all of the foliage. Animals lived here—we'd seen insects, a few deer milling about, and had spotted the occasional degraded carcass picked over by scavengers—but this was not a place where humans could usually be found. Perhaps it would have been more accurate to say that this was a place where humans *didn't belong*.

Thankfully, we'd seen no trace of Eli Lancaster or his men, either. As the hours passed, the odds of our running into the gang of armed men seemed to shrink. It occurred to me that several people could wander these vast woods and never once run into each other. That didn't exactly help our case as we searched for the Occupant, but having one less threat to worry about suited me just fine.

As we paused to discuss our plans moving forward into the evening, I found my gaze wandering to the walls of greenery that pushed in from every side and sensing, in some way, that I was being observed from nearby. I raked the treetops with my gaze, stooped to peer between closely-grown trunks and shoved aside a few branches.

"What's the matter?" asked Jane, noticing my sudden change in demeanor.

I didn't answer her at once. The last mouthful of water I'd sucked down began to gurgle in the pit of my stomach as my senses went haywire. Only moments ago there'd been some birdsong in the air, and the whirring of flying insects had been an omnipresent nuisance.

Now, the woods were completely silent. As if the world were holding its breath, even the breeze paused uncomfortably.

Jake's large hands locked around the straps of his bags till his knuckles went white. He could sense it, too. He sniffed the still air, a bead of sweat rolling off of his chin in the process.

"We're being watched." I hadn't intended to whisper, but my voice had naturally withered to almost nothing in the pervading silence.

Jane held her rifle in both hands, kept it at her side so that she might take aim at the drop of a hat. I wasn't sure if she could feel it, too—the unrelenting pressure of foreign eyes that bored into us from somewhere in the tangle of green—but she stood stock still and waited for me to go on.

"How close are we?" I asked her, my voice still a grainy whisper. "To the mines—to Milsbourne?" The air was thick, suffocating.

Carefully pulling the compass out of her pocket, Jane prepared to do some quick figuring. Instead, she suddenly frowned, staring down at the instrument narrowly.

I glanced over at it and understood why.

The compass wasn't cooperating, the needle edging right to left, right to left, as if being nudged by an invisible finger. I'm no Boy Scout, but I didn't think a compass was supposed to work that way and asked her, "What's wrong with it?"

Rather than answer, she dabbed at her paling face with the back of her hand and returned it to her pocket, brushing aside a nearby branch with the tip of her gun.

That was when I saw it.

Huddled between a number of trees that dwarfed it and left it blackened with shade was a tottering wooden shack. Just how old it was was impossible to say; the bulging, loose-fitting planks that formed its exterior were the kind that had seen at least a hundred springs, a hundred brutal, Michigan winters. The shape of the thing conjured up visions of fron-tier towns—a bygone aesthetic. The real mystery was how it still remained standing after so many years. That its construction had been so sound as to spare its complete ruin over more than a century's existence in these woods never crossed my mind. Rather, it was a kind of stubborn energy, most evident in the harsh angles and singular deep-set window, that must have been responsible for its survival.

I would have liked to ponder its age further, but at that moment my heart found its way into my throat and I felt myself on the verge of illness.

The boxy little structure, glimpsed at a distance of tens of yards, was small and relatively unimposing in and of itself. But through that dark, glassless window, I caught first movement, and then registered an unmistakable humanoid shape stirring just inside it, largely hidden in the murk.

Whoever they were, and whatever it was they were doing inside the shack, their eyes were on us. Of that much I was positive.

"What is that place?" asked Jake. That he said nothing of the person in the window left me dumbstruck. Had he not seem them?

"A little shanty or something." Jane nodded towards it. "Let's have a look."

"W-Wait," I said, grabbing her shoulder and pulling her back a step. "There's someone there." I leaned to one side, squaring the structure in my sights. "There's someone looking at us through the window."

Jane firmed up, brought the gun to her chest. "In the window?"

I nodded. Even as I stood there, still some yards away, I could see the barest outline of a person in that window— the very edges of a face. The distance did nothing to dilute the power of their stare. It wasn't the idea of encountering someone in this remote forest that left my knees shaking. I'd been prepared for the possibility of running into Eli Lancaster or one of his friends; of finding myself face-to-face with the Occupant. What really inspired fear in me was the sight of someone else, someone unexpected, dwelling in that long-forgotten shack. We could have wandered for hours—days—through these woods and never seen another living soul, and yet here we were, approaching a worm-eaten structure as old as the Civil War, and there was someone inside. No, they weren't merely *inside* the place—someone was squirming in that darkness, breathing it in and looking out at us in the same way a nocturnal animal might peer out of a hole in the ground before setting out on its first hunt of the night.

It became clear that my companions weren't seeing what I was seeing. They took a few cautious steps forward, closing the distance, and then took turns giving *me* the side eye. "You sure there's someone in there?" asked Jane.

I gave a quick nod, staying on their heels. The person in the window had receded further into the darkness, but in the shifting light I could still make out the powdery silhouette of an observer. Ten, twenty paces brought them into uncertain relief; I thought I spied a long nose, large, dark eyes, tightly pursed lips. A pale face pinched hastily into a mound of clay.

I clumsily pulled my gun from its holster, the weight of it taking me by surprise once again. I almost dropped it. Holding it low, I followed behind Jane as she hooked towards what appeared to be a doorway set into the side of the structure. Jake spared me a nervous look, probably wondering if I intended to use the gun on whatever lurked inside the shack.

Like me, he was wondering if I had the balls to shoot a living thing.

If I had what it took to kill Elizabeth.

All you have to do is point and squeeze the trigger, I reminded myself, making an effort to suppress my breathing.

Jane paused outside the entrance to the shack, gave me a quick nod and then—gun at the ready and finger seeking out the trigger—she stepped inside.

11

There wasn't a lot of ground to cover in the little shack, and even before Jane broke out one of the flashlights and angrily canvassed the space, it was clear from the doorway that there was no one inside.

I couldn't explain what I'd seen—what I'd *thought* I'd seen—but that the others resented me for my frequent false alarms was becoming clear. "Not a soul," muttered Jane, casting her light into the corners, across the battered floors. It was unlikely that the warped planks would support our weight, and so we didn't go very far, lingering near the door. Much of the space was hung in spider's silk. The roof had partially caved and the branch of a tree jutted a few feet into the shanty by way of the breach. In a corner of the room, piled in what seemed to me a natural fashion, were the bones of an animal who'd wandered in and died. I couldn't tell what kind, though in that moment the sight of any bones—any reminder of death, really—was not at all comforting.

"Was it Elizabeth?" asked Jake, stepping back outside

and looking eagerly about the shack. "Do you think it was her?"

I rubbed at my face, a dull ache forming behind my eyes. The person I'd seen had been hard to make out from a distance, and I'd lost sight of them completely as we'd edged towards the door. Now that I'd had a look inside, I felt silly, but had you asked me only moments ago I'd have sworn there was someone standing just inside the window, glaring out at us. "It's the Occupant," I said. "It must be tampering with my perception... making me see things that aren't there."

Jane arched a brow, lowering her gun as she left the shack. "I'm not so sure about that." Leaning forward to look me in the eye, she frowned. "You're jumpy, paranoid. I know what I said before, but the Occupant doesn't have to do anything—you're doing a fine job of keeping yourself frightened."

It was true. I'd been uneasy ever since starting this hike, and the shadowed woods only made it easier to mistake everyday sights for something ominous. "I'm sorry. I'll try and rein it in. But I..."

She motioned to the shack. "You *thought* you saw someone inside. We had a look. It's empty. Get over it."

Jake chimed in, looking past the shack with a furrowed brow. "So, what is this thing? Just an old cabin? Are we in Milsbourne now? Have we finally made it?"

Looking down at her compass, which was still acting strangely, Jane set down her bag and hurriedly walked the perimeter of the leaning structure. "I dunno. Didn't see any welcome signs along the way, did *you?*" she mocked. "We should be getting close, but I'm not sure we've made it yet. Of course, with the compass having gone to shit, I don't even know if we're heading the right way."

Jake tensed. "W-We're lost?"

She clicked her tongue, threw out a hand as if to silence him, but it was pretty clear she was getting agitated because she'd lost her bearings. "Not quite lost, no. Just... wandering a little."

"Oh, we're *wandering* now? That's cool. I'm glad we found some time to take in this lush scenery," I said. "Why don't we start looking for some moss or animal prints. Those might lead us to civilization, yeah?"

Jane fumed, stopping to jab me in the gut with an extended finger. "Who the fuck are you? Percy Fawcett?" She spit into the sprawling bushes, hands on her hips. "Give me a damn second, all right? We're a little ways from the mines yet. We haven't really even hit any hills so far. The way's been flat, and until just a bit ago I knew we were heading due north. That tells me we've got some ground left to cover, but..." She took a moment to kick the outside of the ramshackle tenement. "We're finding some old buildings. That's a good sign."

When we'd taken another short break—this time for the sake of our minds, rather than our bodies—Jake and I followed Jane as she struck past the shack and dove once more into what she believed was the northern wilderness. We were only some minutes gone from the little shanty when I turned and found it completely blocked from view by the trees. It had appeared suddenly, almost out of thin air, and had been tucked back into the woods to lie in wait. More than a hundred years had gone by since anyone had lived in it, and another hundred years would likely pass before anyone else would stumble upon it again. Like some rarely seen animal, the shack resumed its clandestine existence, disappearing into the scenery as we moved on.

Though she was an experienced hiker and knew the

area well, the forest seemed to be getting to Jane. Several minutes passed and she began to curse the heat, to complain about the bugs and the sometimes discordant songs of the "damned birds". Jake had largely fallen back to the rear position and was taking special care to look for other structures hidden amongst the trees.

I was back inside my own head, wondering whether I could really trust myself—and whether or not my mindset was a liability for the whole group. It was possible—quite likely—that the Occupant was playing tricks on me, singling me out as a weak link the way it had consistently done on our way into Michigan. Though the entity had once paid Jane's head a visit, she wasn't falling prey to hallucinations, and neither was Jake. Only I kept mistaking commonplace sights for leering specters—only I was assailed by the feeling of foreign eyes.

Jake brushed aside a tall, wavy thing—a bush or over-grown weed—and broke from the pack. "Get a load of this," he said, kneeling down.

Jane and I turned to join him, spotting what looked to be another small shack. This one, though, had not been spared by the years and sat in a weathered heap, flattened. The agent responsible for its collapse, the trunk of a large, light-ning-struck tree, still rested at the top of the mound, and had seemingly become cemented to the stuff of the shack by moss, dirt and gossamer webbing.

"Another one," marveled Jake. "We must be getting close."

Nodding, Jane grunted and urged us onward.

We stepped past the wreckage and kept on, Jane taking a token glance down at her broken compass and narrowly avoiding the urge to throw it to the ground.

We weren't five minutes from the site of the flattened

shack when we arrived at what looked to be an old well. It was comprised of flat, grungy stones, a few of which were missing. Any bucket or cover for the thing had been lost long ago.

This, coupled with the shacks we were discovering every mile or so, certainly looked like the remnants of an old mining town.

I approached the well, placing a hand against the grimy exterior stones, and looked inside. From down below, brought into view by a faint veil of sunlight from overhead, a pale, distorted face gawked back up at me. I startled, managed to knock one of the stones into the well in my fright, and watched as the ghastly face—my own, thrown out of proportion in the water's reflection—broke into a series of ripples. The well was rather full, likely due to the recent rains. A stench that reminded me of a flooded basement wafted up from the opening.

"What's the matter?" asked Jake.

I shook my head, said nothing. *You're losing it, man. Hold yourself together.*

"We're getting close now." Jane stamped the ground lightly with the sole of her boot. "You feel the change in elevation? We're heading into the hills now. Which means we're probably only a few miles from the mines." She looked up at the sky, which was only growing dimmer by the moment, and whistled. "Don't know if we're going to get there before dark, though. And I sure as hell don't want to wander these woods in the dead of night."

"Are we going to set up camp?" I asked. Though the thought of sharing a tent with these two in the humid woods didn't exactly appeal, the thought of laying down to sleep, of blocking out the forest scenery for a time and giving my worried mind a rest, sounded great.

"Not just yet," she said. "We'll go a little further, see what we find. Maybe once we get up to the top of a hill."

Leaning forward to center my load on my back, I followed the other two and felt the ground swell gradually beneath my feet. It was time to climb.

IT WAS difficult to say for sure in the failing light, but I thought I saw something pointing up through the trees. I didn't say anything at first, still unsure whether I could trust my senses, and instead kept an eye on the dark shape that seemed to cut through the woods in the distance. It didn't look like a tree. It looked like the top of a building—possibly a steeple.

"I wish we'd started earlier," said Jane as we trudged on. We weren't going to make it much further today and she was absorbed in searching for a good place to pitch our tent. We'd need a clearing of some kind, a patch of dry land that was open enough for us to set up the large tent and have a bit of room for a fire besides. Considering the density of the woods, that was a pretty tall order.

At one point, a large squirrel came darting out of a gnarled bush and scampered directly past Jake's feet, sending him into a panic. He wobbled, loosed a yelp and fell on his ass, giving Jane and I the only hit of genuine levity we'd gotten all day. I helped him up, then turned my gaze upward to a break in the foliage where, sure enough, the dark, angular shape still jutted into the sky. Not wanting to piss off my companions, I pointed casually at the sight. "Do you guys see that? It looks like there's some sort of building over there. I think I can see the top of it."

The two of them studied the canopy in turn and zeroed in on it. "I think I see it. Is that a church steeple?" asked Jake.

I sighed, relieved that this wasn't one of my delusions. There was something substantial waiting for us just ahead —possibly a landmark we could use in determining our exact location.

Jane nodded. "Looks like it." Pacing forward, she continued searching for a decent spot to pitch the tent. "We can worry about that tomorrow. We may very well be close, but the sun's about to drop out of the sky. Better to hurry and get a camp ready." We were at the top of a hill—one in a series of many we'd climbed in the past half hour—and were able to find a small clearing at the bottom, a few hundred feet away. The spot, largely clear of trees, was noticeably brighter for the lack of growth, and as we drew closer it appeared drier, too.

"So, do you know a building like that?" asked Jake. "A building with a tall steeple?"

Jane shook her head, focusing instead on the clearing.

"Do you know where we're at right now?" continued Jake.

"Yeah," was all Jane said.

Jake and I exchanged a glance, had a brief, silent conversation, and it was clear that neither of us really believed her.

Sliding down a particularly steep bit of the hill, Jane steadied herself against a tree and marched into the clearing, hefting her bags off to one side and letting them drop to the grass. Mashing at the ground with her feet, she nodded agreeably. "It's dry enough." She looked upward, studied the darkening sky. "And not a moment too soon. Let's get the camp set up."

It became clear rather quickly that I was a complete waste of space when it came to setting up a camp. I'd never done it before. Except for watching shows like *Man vs. Wild* on TV and living vicariously through Bear Grylls, I'd never seen a proper camp put together. I could count on one hand how many times I'd *actually* slept outdoors in my life, and most of those times had involved me passing out on frat house lawns, drunk.

Enlisting Jake to help her get the stakes into the ground and the tent thrown together, Jane ordered me to gather wood for a campfire—a task so simple that even I couldn't mess it up. "We need dry material. Some thin, some thick. See what you can find."

Setting down my bags, I started wandering about the borders of the clearing, looking through the tall grass and picking up twigs and branches, which I broke up into more manageable pieces. Tucking the small load under my arm, I continued searching for tinder until I had trouble keeping hold of it all and started back towards the nearly-pitched tent to drop it off. The sky was losing color fast, shifting from a warm gold to a cold, suffocating blue. The breeze in this spot was almost pleasant, cooler than it had been earlier in the day. If the temperature and humidity dropped, maybe I'd manage some sleep after all.

While walking back into the woods to seek out more firewood, I caught sight once more of that sharp, steeple shape in the distance. It couldn't have been far. From where I stood it looked perhaps half a mile away, though hours walking in the woods and the changes in the elevation had taught me that estimating distance in such a setting was more than a little difficult. Maybe it really was a church, another building left miraculously intact from the days of the miners. I wondered what shape it would be in, whether we'd learn anything from it.

Milsbourne. The abandoned mining town that didn't

exist on any modern map. The settlement that'd been reduced to a mere footnote in obscure historical texts, and which seemed to be the place where this nightmare had really begun. Every major player in this tangled web had some connection to Milsbourne—a place that'd largely emptied out in the 1870's. Corvine had known about it. The historian Jamieson Monroe had sought it out—and had disappeared after returning to it. Our dear Elizabeth had been born in this area.

I pulled aside a knot of weeds and picked up a nice, thick branch. Beside it, sticking out of the grass awkwardly, was a white, rigid mass. I knelt down to have a look, and then dropped the firewood I'd been carrying in abject horror.

It was a severed hand. Where it had been wrenched from the wrist—the incredible damage to the blood-damp stump told me it had been *pulled* from the forearm with great force—a tangled mass of clots and severed vessels lay scattered like ribbons.

I held my breath, closed my eyes, tried counting to ten.

You're imagining it. You're being paranoid again. Get ahold of yourself.

I opened my eyes.

It was still there, the fingers splayed.

I rose to my feet and fought the urge to throw up. Shaking my head, I looked back towards the clearing, where Jane was putting the finishing touches on the tent and Jake was drinking from a gallon jug of water.

It's not real. It's not real, damn it!

From behind me there came a sound that frightened me to my core—the kind of sound that millions of years of evolution had programmed human minds to react to. The low, hateful growling of an animal. I turned slowly, spying a dark grey paw, then another, emerging from a thicket of cedars.

A wolf.

I froze, and the beast stared me down. Its teeth—sharp, yellowed, numerous—made an appearance as it loosed another of its growls. The beast crept towards me, was certainly within pouncing distance, when it edged to one side and, sniffing the grass, took up the severed hand in its spittle-flecked maw. Squeezing the pale morsel between its teeth—the fingers almost seeming to writhe and the wrist portion dribbling half-coagulated blood onto the grass—the wolf veered back towards the treeline and vanished into the woods.

Jane, who'd been about to ask me for more wood, had noticed the wolf moments before its departure and rushed over with her gun in hand. "The hell you doing over here, staring at that thing? It could have mauled you. Are you stupid?"

My heart thumped in my chest, the rhythm going a bit haywire. I felt short of breath and the edges of my vision grew dark for a moment. I hadn't been staring at the wolf, exactly. Rather, I'd been staring at the hand it'd gobbled up.

The gore-slick hand in the grass had been real.

I hadn't hallucinated it.

The sickness came. Precious water and flecks of trail mix sloshed into the grass as I wretched.

"Fuck," muttered Jane. "What's the matter with you?"

I pointed to the blood in the grass, but couldn't explain myself for some minutes, when the urge to heave had finally passed.

12

"There was a hand?" asked Jane, sitting me down just inside the tent.

My palms stuck to the plasticky material as I shifted my weight, nodding. "A severed hand, yeah. I don't know whose it was, but it was fairly fresh. Still bleeding a little."

Jake, white in the face, was squatting beside the meager pile of wood I'd gathered, toying nervously with sticks. He pinched one between his fingers, asking, "Whose could it have been?"

Jane was dissecting me with her gaze. It was clear she didn't fully believe me, and after my previous mishaps, I couldn't fault her for her skepticism.

"Look, you saw the wolf, right?" I challenged. "Unless the wolf was hallucinating too, it snatched up that hand and ran off into the woods. The blood's still out there. You saw it for yourself."

She nodded, casting her surgical gaze towards the tree-line and offering a heavy sigh. "We can't stay here. If there's a body nearby, then it's going to attract all kinds of unwanted attention. And where there's one wolf, there's usually more. A lot more."

"W-Was it a man's hand?" asked Jake, bottom lip quivering just a touch. "Or was it a woman's?"

"Gee, let me think. You know, the nails were done in Urban Plum polish, and their moisturizer game was definitely on-point. I could have sat there shaking that hand forever," I scoffed. "Shut the hell up, already. It wasn't your girlfriend's hand, I'm pretty confident of that. If anything... your darling Elizabeth is probably the one that tore it off of someone to begin with."

"It's possible that the girl got to Lancaster's party," said Jane. "They probably came into the woods, met the thing and had a fight. If there are chunks of those guys laying around in the woods, then the outcome of said fight is pretty damn clear."

"We should keep going," I said. "We should go a little further, while there's still a bit of light out. Maybe we'll find some of them—alive—in that building up ahead, with the steeple."

Jane crinkled her nose. "No. We should move our camp, but... we don't want to get any closer to this thing so close to nightfall." She worked her jaw in her hand, clearly conflicted. She wanted to uproot the tent and move out of this area where bears and wolves were likely to come poking around for more scraps, and yet there was nowhere for us to relocate to. This particular clearing had been the only one we'd encountered for miles that was really suited to being a campsite. Heading towards the steepled building—closer to what we presumed was Milsbourne—was a suicide mission to her mind, what with the Occupant running around. But to stay at the camp and wait for the wolves to make a reappearance was equally reckless.

"If we find one of them—one of Eli's guys—maybe they can help us. What do you think? There's power in numbers." I nodded to the steeple. "Let's check it out. If it's a problem, we can hightail it back here, to camp. It can't be very far. And depending on how sound the building is, we may even be able to get some height and survey the area from above."

Jane grimaced. "Doesn't seem like larger numbers helped the owner of that lost hand too much." Despite her reticence, it was clear she saw no other way forward. We needed to figure out what lay ahead, have a look at this landmark that was visible through the trees. Urging us to bring our flashlights along, she hatched a plan. "We'll go on a little further, see what's up. Maybe we'll leave our camp here, maybe we won't, depending on what we find."

I nodded. "Is it safe for us to leave this stuff here unattended?" I thought back to my Cavalier, to the Occupant's penchant for torching necessary supplies, and wondered if it wouldn't be wise for one of us, maybe Jake, to hang back.

She shook her head. "If we split up, there goes the 'power in numbers'. We stick together."

With flashlights in hand, the three of us left the camp behind and started into the dusky woods, keeping an eye on the dark steeple looming over the tops of the trees. It was an easy thing to lose sight of, as the canopy often blocked our view of the sky—of anything other than foliage—but we managed to keep on in its general direction, leaning on the last vestiges of daylight to guide us.

We'd have made it there a lot sooner, but we stumbled upon a few things that'd given us pause.

Jane's flashlight illuminated something dangling from a tree branch, swaying in the wind, that I initially took for a strange vine. We had only to take a few steps forward to realize that wasn't the case at all. We were looking at a length of *meat*, the human kind, which had been left strewn in the treetops by what seemed a freak accident.

Or, maybe, it'd been left intentionally.

The carnage—a pale, bumpy section of human intestine, still glistening with red—was crawling with flies. Whether it belonged to the same person who'd lost their hand we couldn't say; I find it rather hard to identify someone based on the wrinkles of their viscera. Suffice it to say, the three of us took turns studying it in the glow of our flashlights and gave it a wide berth as we staggered on, retching. Even Jane was bothered at the sight, spitting repeatedly onto the ground as if to preempt a wave of vomit.

We'd gone only ten or twenty feet further when Jake stopped in his tracks and glanced up at something sitting in the crook of a half-bald pine. He lost his balance, bumping into me with his linebacker frame, and nearly toppled the both of us. His voice was trapped in his throat for a moment, but once his terror grew large enough to overcome the hitch in his windpipe, he whimpered loudly.

A man's head had been set atop one of the lowermost branches of that tree, balanced against the trunk. The eyes had been taken, leaving only dark hollows that teemed with clots. The mouth, mangled so that it might sit wider than was usually possible, sat open with serpentine unhingedness. It was a hideous sight, the work of something truly barbarous, and yet there appeared to be a reason behind this desecration.

The carefully-placed and mutilated head was a sign, a sign that read: "Turn back from here" in a language that all men—and most animals—are proficient in: Death.

And how I would have liked to heed that warning. I trust that my companions would have, too.

But we were in the middle of the forest. Night would soon be upon us.

There was nowhere to run. One could race for miles—for almost an entire day—through this wilderness and still never find a paved road.

Never in my life—and that includes our evening spent at Chaythe Asylum—had I ever felt so hopelessly trapped as this. The dangers of hunting the Occupant were no longer abstract, theoretical. The entity posed a clear and present danger, and had no trouble in flaunting its talents for killing. The trail of carnage would lead us, probably, to a face-to-face meeting with that terror, and even if we'd wanted to, we'd stranded ourselves in the middle of a vast wilderness with no easy exit plan. We weren't even sure of our exact position—Jane, our guide, was navigating mostly blind due to the compass's malfunction.

Jake regained his balance, but his lips quivered so hard I thought he might end up with a permanent stutter. "T-That guy... was he one of Lancaster's friends?"

Jane, steadying herself, palmed the sweat from her face and pointed at the severed head with her gun. "See that, kid? Get a good look at it. Who do you think did that, huh? Who's responsible for that, do you think?" She looked at him expectantly, wanting to treat this as a teaching moment. "This is what your girlfriend has been up to lately. This is what she's capable of. Still think the best thing is to try and talk with her?"

Jake knew damn well how that head had gotten there, of course. Shifting uncomfortably, he looked back in the direction we'd come. "Maybe... maybe we should go back to the camp," he suggested. "Going any further would be..."

Jane marched on, unwilling to listen any further.

I followed, knowing we were damned either way, and

carefully unholstered my gun, holding it in my hand like I'd seen characters on TV police procedurals do. Before long, Jake was at my heels, his flashlight sending a quaking beam of yellow light at everything he pointed to.

The sun slipped out of the sky completely, leaving the heavens a back-lit navy color. There was a change in the wind—it felt colder, made me shiver—though I couldn't be sure whether the shivering was truly on account of the breeze.

The gun in my hand felt like shitty insurance. I'd never fired it before, wasn't sure I'd be able to hit a damn thing even if my life depended on it. And anyway, walking through these dense woods, where we knew Elizabeth to lurk, it felt like we were walking through a field full of land-mines. I'd seen her strength, her speed, since taking on the Occupant. The monstrosity could steamroll us if it wanted to, and could be hiding behind literally any tree.

I thought there were mushrooms or wildflowers scattered through the undergrowth ahead, but canvassing the ground with my light, I found myself hopping around to avoid bits of human flesh. There was an ear, partially buried in the soil; several teeth; a pair of eyes, whose size and coloration led me to believe they'd come from two distinct—and unwilling—donors. Tree trunks within arm's reach were dashed with streaks of dried blood, as if major vessels had been tapped in a sudden, violent attack. I heard Jake gag, and he buried his nose and mouth in the crook of his arm to block out the gradually intensifying smell of meat and blood left to warm in the humid woods.

We were descending a hill, and at the bottom of it the trees seemed to thin out very slightly.

The carnage did not, however.

Swatches of intestine, like so many links of red sausage

garland, festooned the trees. Another decapitated and disfigured head, this one with longer hair that had been tied onto a low-hanging branch so as to make it hang, stared at us with coagulated, empty sockets. Its lower jaw had been pulled off completely—a thing which I accidentally trampled underfoot—and the tongue, wearing a black carpet of flies, seemed to faintly sway, like a beckoning finger.

It was the entrance to Hell itself.

Stunned into silence by these sights, we emerged into something like a clearing. The trees grew further apart here, and up ahead, taking advantage of the space, was a structure much larger than any we'd hitherto seen in the woods. It was boxy and wide, its exterior made of loose hanging boards stained grey by the elements. Its peak, which tapered into a shabby steeple, and a faded concrete plaque commemorating its date of construction—1849—confirmed our earlier suspicions. It was an old church. The plaque read *Anima Christi*, in faded characters. *"Soul of Christ"*, if my college Latin could still be trusted. Aside from the date, there was one other bit of text I could still make out on the stone slab. *Milsbourne, Michigan.*

The building, constructed before the Civil War had even taken place, and some twenty years before the reported abandonment of Milsbourne, was still standing by some miracle. Perhaps the faithful would attribute its longevity to divine intervention, though I have to admit our dire surroundings made it harder than usual for me to pour my faith into anything divine.

But the sight of this church made one thing clear.

We'd arrived.

We took turns looking down at the plaque and pacing cautiously around the exterior of the building. There looked to be only a single entrance, a dark hole where doors had once stood that now looked like a yawning, toothless mouth. Some twenty or more feet above this opening were two broken windows that, in their day, might have been made of stained glass. Like the heads we'd seen positioned throughout the woods, the church looked out blankly into the forest, the broken windows like black, empty sockets.

There was more. Left around the building—in disarray or as intended decoration, I couldn't say—were scraps of men. The ground was dark with blood in several spots, and not far from these clotted puddles, whole, disembodied limbs could be found. Tattered clothing, smooth pieces of tissue likely taken from major organs, and more were stepped over as we made our silent examination of the church.

Meeting the others back out front, near the plaque, I shook my head and said in a low voice, as if a Mass were going on inside, "We're here. This is Milsbourne. It seems the Occupant beat us here, though. Do you think any of Lancaster's crew survived?"

Jake had barely regained his legs. It was clear he'd never seen this kind of butchery in real life. No one outside of war was likely to see this level of savagery, for that matter, and the state of our surroundings made *me* feel like I'd stepped into a Romero flick. He was taking it harder than Jane and I however, becoming uncommunicative, probably because he was coming to terms with the fact that Elizabeth had done this.

I tried not to focus too much on that aspect. I'd seen a lot of shit recently, but the idea of Elizabeth Morrissey tearing apart a pack of roughs like the ones that'd shown up at Jane's door the night before still boggled the mind.

Jane smoothed back her sweat-slick hair and panned slowly across treeline from which we'd emerged. "I don't know who I'd feel more sorry for," she began. "The victims or the survivors who'd have to go on living with memories of what went on here." Her jaw tensed. "It was a bloodbath. I doubt anyone managed to get out alive. If they did, they're probably out there in the woods somewhere, dead or dying from blood loss." She bent down to examine a drying puddle of blood, several small insects squirming in the red soup.

"Well, either way, this is Milsbourne. We've made it." I nodded towards the entrance of the church. "Shall we have a look inside?" It occurred to me that I'd been clutching the gun in my hand for quite a while, and my arm was getting sore. I switched hands, flexing my fingers. "The Occupant may still be around here."

"Wolves, mountain lions, the Occupant. There's something waiting to kill us around every corner," said Jane, gaining her feet. "We'll have a quick look. After that, we need to rush back to camp. We don't want to get caught out here in the open until we know what the girl's game is. She led us out here, left us quite the trail to follow, but whatever awaits us—"

There was a stirring from somewhere inside the church. A shifting of weight, a vague thumping, drifted from the open doorway.

The sound was like a slap in the face. We all stood bolt upright, weapons in hand, and held our breaths.

Is the Occupant still in there? Has it been waiting for us inside? Jane led us towards the doorway, her finger resting on the trigger, and I could't help but think to myself that a bear or mountain lion would be a far more welcome sight within the church than the thing we'd come to find. Wild animals are capable of savagery, but they only utilize it as a means of survival.

The Occupant had made a game out of killing, and was far more proficient at it than any other creature in this forest.

Jake and I took over flashlight duty, and I held my gun out in front of me, ready to squeeze the trigger at the first sign of movement. We stepped into the doorway and were greeted by an impressive darkness. From this darkness Jake and I dredged up a scene of utter chaos with our lights. Toppled and broken wooden pews; rotten hymnals on the verge of disintegration, breaks in the roof where hints of fresh moonlight seeped in. It might have been God's house, once, but the church of Milsbourne was only a suitable home for spiders at this point. The gaps between many of the wall planks were filled in with decades of gossamer grout.

And there was blood.

Just inside the door, a grayish red for the addition of dust, was a small pool of blood. Further in, seeming to form a staggered trail, were stout rivulets that were rather fresh and vibrant against the light, standing out like crimson beads. Ahead of those, beside what appeared to be a simple altar towards the back, were a couple of smeared hand-prints, as might be made by a man fleeing on his hands and knees.

The maker of those handprints was curled into a fetal position just ahead, a piece of rebar buried in the side of his skull and his thinking parts still oozing through the tremendous wound.

The stirring reached our ears a second time from the direction of the altar. I pointed my gun and flashlight straight ahead, and very nearly pulled the trigger out of impulse. Jane did the same, and stepping past Jake and I, she growled at the figure who could now be seen to lurk at the foot of the altar. "Hands up."

The figure at the altar turned around very slightly, and suddenly I blanked.

This wasn't what I'd been expecting.

13

"Eli Lancaster?" uttered Jane in disbelief. She lowered her gun just a tad and took a few paces towards the man, whose face was damp with blood and sweat. He was clutching at his upper arms, and had been kneeling at the altar in a huddled, shuddering mass. "What... what are you doing there?"

The man, wearing only a pair of jeans and pressing a palm against what looked to be a serious wound on his right flank, did not respond. Instead, he sobbed, and a gasping, terrible noise that he'd kept bottled up for too long burst from his throat. His fingertips were pale as he clutched the wound and attempted to keep himself from bleeding out. The man I'd seen at Jane's trailer had been large and imposing. Confident. Eli Lancaster, then, was nothing but a memory now, because the man who cowered in the beams of our flashlights, weeping, was nothing at all like him. They had the same face, the same frame, but this man had been broken.

Jake tried calling out to him, in vain. "S-Sir? Mr. Lancaster? Are you... are you all right?"

Lancaster turned back to the altar, tightening his hold on his own body, and breathed out what sounded like a whispered prayer. A stream of blood dripped between his fingers and hit the floor, resulting in a barely audible splash like a leaky tap.

Remaining silent, Jane approached the altar and knelt down within arm's reach of the man. Waving to Jake and I, she kept the gun fixed on him and had us bring the light a little closer. From there she was able to see the extent of Eli's wound. He only seemed to have one, except for a number of bumps and scrapes, but it was a gusher. Deep and ragged, whatever had gotten him had cleaved through layers of skin and muscle alike. Though I couldn't be sure, I thought I saw the head of a dark organ pulsing beneath his palm as he labored to keep it inside of him. I fell onto my ass and averted my gaze, and was almost carried off on a riptide of nausea when Jane spoke once more.

"Eli," she said, "What happened?" She looked around the church, studied the punctured roof, the other side of the altar, the entrance.

"What happened to you and your friends?" asked Jake. "Did... did the wolves get to you?"

At this, Eli finally replied. "What did this is no longer here," he said in a frail voice, like he couldn't take a full breath. "But I tell you one thing... it wasn't a damn wolf."

Jane nodded, having guessed long ago what was responsible for all of the carnage, and placed a hand upon his shoulder. "Let's have a better look at that wound in your side," she said. "Come away from there, let's get you patched up. We have a first aid kit with us." The awful frown on her face as she glanced down at the wound—and the pool of blood Eli was sitting in—told me that it was much worse than it looked from where I was sitting, and that nothing in the first aid kit was going to do anything for him.

"No," gasped Eli, balling his hand into a fist and nearly inserting it into the wound like a knot of gauze. "I've... I've come to make my final peace. There ain't nothing to be done. I just..." He made an effort to breathe deeply, but he couldn't get the air into him. His lungs sounded so wet they may as well have been full of chowder. "I pray that God will forgive me... forgive my line..."

"Forgive you for what?" I asked, letting the gun rest in my lap. I licked my lips, the air tasting like a mix of antique mall dust, rain and blood.

Eli spared me a narrow glance, turning his head ever so slightly. "The curse of my forebears..." he said with a wince.

The curse of his forebears? I thought. *What's that supposed to mean?* Before I could question him further, Jane spoke up.

"Where has it gone?" she asked. "The thing that did this to you? Where did it go, Eli?"

The man shook his head, taking his time to reply. "It's gone now..." he began before a fit of coughing overtook him.

Jake didn't wait for the hacking to cease and manhandled the guy, tugging him off of his knees. Eli's hand slipped and a torrent of gore pulsed forth from the awful wound on his flank. I only glimpsed it for a minute in the beam of my flashlight—he was quick to reapply his hand to it—but the wound, strange though it was, looked to me like a deep bite mark. The outer edge had about it the sort of ragged character that I'd seen in a severe dog bite as a child. When teeth meet flesh, they have a way of tearing the meat away that you can't reproduce with a bladed weapon. I was chilled by the implication but didn't say anything as Jake shook him down. "What do you mean, it's *gone* now?" he demanded, looking straight into the man's vacant eyes. "Did you hurt her? Kill her?"

Slumping back onto one of his elbows, chest rising and falling as he tried to catch his breath, Eli shook his head. "N-No, it's waiting for you."

"Where?" asked Jane, shooting Jake daggers and pulling him carefully away.

Eli grit his teeth as a fresh wave of pain coursed through him. Looking upward, through the break in the roof, he stared at the starlit sky. "You won't have to wonder where it's gone," he coughed. "It'll come for you... all of you... one by one." His lips grew wet with a sheen of bloody mucous. "During the day, it hides in the Earth like an animal. But at night, it moves as it pleases. It'll be out. Soon." He blinked tiredly at the night sky, spoke dreamily, like a father dozing off while trying to tell his kids a bedtime story.

The story was left unfinished. Those were the last words that Eli Lancaster ever spoke. Having lost too much blood and drawn too little breath, he let go of the wound in his side and eased himself onto his back, dying moments later with his eyes wide open.

"Hold on, stay with me," said Jane, trying to shake some life into the man. Realizing it was no use, she carefully stood and leveled the rifle at her side. "Goddammit, Eli."

The three of us said nothing for a long while, merely standing in the dark, silent church as we processed Eli's final words. *It's waiting for you. It'll come for you. All of you. One by one. It hides in the Earth like an animal by day, moves at night. You won't have to wonder where it's gone. It'll come for you.* I couldn't make heads or tails of Eli's parting remarks, and in any other situation I'd have convinced myself that these had merely been the ramblings of a dying man, left insane by fear and blood loss. Eli's description of his killer differed somewhat from the Occupant's habits. And then he'd gone on about his "family's curse". What role did the Lancaster lineage play in this?

"What was he talking about?" asked Jake, gripping his Maglite like a club and stepping over Eli's body. "What hides in the Earth... and comes out at night?"

Jane acted like she didn't hear him. She made certain not to step in the pool of Eli's blood and then walked slowly towards the church entrance, her boots thumping on the dirty stone floors.

Jake and I followed her out into the night, nerves still ratcheted. "He talked about a curse—a family curse. How did the Lancasters get mixed up in all of this?" I asked.

Jane simply shook her head. "Why don't you go in there and ask him? He was probably the only man alive who could answer that question."

The woods around us felt unnaturally still. The wind stopped blowing for several beats and a stifling, weighty quietude settled upon us like a sandbag. I felt like the gravity on Earth had just doubled in strength as I fell into step behind Jane. She was heading back up the hill, looking to return to camp.

"What are we going to do now?" asked Jake. I thought I heard his teeth chattering.

"We're going back to camp," replied Jane. "To wait."

Jake looked to her with wide eyes. "Wait for what?"

Without turning to face him, Jane pushed through the treeline and focused on climbing the hill. "According to Eli, we're going to have a visitor pretty soon."

As we walked, I thought back to the wound on Eli's abdomen. "Did you get a look at that wound? I didn't get too close, but if you ask me, it looked almost like something took a bite out of him. Real deep. Teeth marks."

"Maybe," was all Jane said.

"Like, an animal bite? You think Eli got bit by an animal?" asked Jake. The hint of hope in his voice—the hope of finding a scapegoat for all of this carnage that would exonerate his girlfriend—was grating to hear. "What kind of animal do you think it was? A bear? A wolf, maybe?"

"Don't get your hopes up," I replied. "It's too early to rule anything out, but... he said it wasn't a wolf that did it. If he'd stayed alive just a few more minutes then maybe we'd have gotten him to talk a little sense. He was unclear." I tried picturing Elizabeth Morrissey as the apex predator responsible for delivering that mortal wound—her orange hair soaked in blood, a hunk of pulsing, living human flesh between her teeth—but it was too grotesque and unbelievable to imagine. "What do you think, Jane?"

She shook her head. "The only thing I know is that I don't know anything." Jane sighed, reaching the top of the hill before us, and stepping around some of the human confetti we'd seen on our way to the church. If there was any silver lining to be found in the massacre of those men, it was that the positioning of their entrails made it much easier for us to find our way back to camp.

"Are we going to move our camp?" Jake stared down at the meaty wreckage with a shudder. "Is it safe for us to camp so close to all of these bodies? I thought you said that wild animals might be a problem..."

"There's nowhere safe in these woods," Jane shot back. "I thought you knew that coming in. There's nowhere to run to, no escape. And the last thing I'm worried about is a wild animal. Animals respond to bullets, kid. What we're after... or what's after us... Well, just ask Eli Lancaster how that worked out for him. No sense in moving the camp. Trouble's on its way no matter where we go." In our silence, Jane continued, thinking aloud. "I wonder if we can't find some way out of here. There might be a shortcut... if I can just get the compass to work, I can try and get us going south, maybe southeast. There are some major roads if you go far enough that way..."

To hear Jane of all people consider fleeing the woods just about robbed me of all my fight. Despite the lack of any present danger, my heart began to skip around in my chest. Panic set in, icing up my limbs and sending a shiver down my spine. The air was still humid, but with the sun having gone down the forest's warmth was beginning to wane. As a result, I thought I could make out small pockets of fog forming here and there, hanging where the trees were most dense.

We made it back to camp and were surprised to find nothing out of place. For once, fate had been kind to us. We picked up some of the wood I'd dropped and carried it to the middle of the clearing, however Jane soon decided it wasn't worth starting a fire and urged us to head into the tent. She advised us to eat, drink and sleep, though it soon became apparent that none of us could stand the thought of food after all we'd seen.

"We'll sleep in two-hour shifts," she said. "You two sleep first. If something happens, I'll wake you. One of us has to be up at all times." Jane looked to me sternly. "Don't leave the tent. If you *think* you see something, tell me. But don't go off on your own."

We sat cross-legged in the tent, each of us taking a corner. There was more than enough room for us to stretch out, and the grass in this particular spot made sleeping on the ground more comfortable than I'd expected. Jake was the first to drift off. His body had shut down on him after carrying the bulk of our things during the day's hike.

Jane and I, though, would need to work towards sleep.

The tent was practically pitch dark. I couldn't see my hand in front of my face, but from certain of the seams around the zippered entrance, traces of moonlight did make it through. I stared upward, hands on my belly, and tried to calm myself by doing some deep breathing. "Jane," I said quietly, "you're freezing me out. What do you think about all of this—the things Eli said, what happened to his men? What's going on in these woods and how is it tied to his bloodline?"

Jane was pensive for a while. I could hear her shift as she tucked her knees beneath her chin and exhaled. "I don't know," she replied. Her voice, in the darkness, was quiet and soothing. It reminded me in a small way of my grandmother's voice. When I was little, I spent a lot of time being babysat by my grandmother while my parents worked. Some nights, she'd tuck me in and read me a story. If I had trouble sleeping, she'd sit at the foot of my bed, in the dark, watching over me until I managed to drift off. Something about the current situation, strange through it was, reminded me of those long-passed days. I almost thought to tell her so, but knew Jane would just laugh and call me an idiot.

"The Occupant was inside of me, and it taught me about the nature of life and death. But I don't know everything there is to know. I don't know its history. It's possible that the Occupant was here on Earth before I came into the picture. And perhaps, when my uncle was busy groping for someone to speak to in the world beyond, he got its attention—got tangled in the web. The drugs, the experiments... my uncle opened the door and let it into the world. That's what I've always believed. If he'd never done that, then I doubt we'd be here in the woods, searching for the girl. But somehow, Eli and his ancestors seem to have a history with it, so it's possible that the thing was here long before that. Maybe the Occupant originally came from out here..." She trailed off.

"OK, so maybe your uncle wasn't the one who *opened* the door. Maybe he's just the one who showed it the way." I actually managed a yawn. "Question is, how does one *close* the door? Is it possible?"

"Get some sleep," she said, effectively ending the conversation.

I rolled onto my side and worked on doing just that. It took some time, but as I closed my eyes and stretched out across the plastic floor, feeling the tall grass shift beneath me, my mind and body seemingly got together, realized how damn sore I was for the half-day death march we'd made, and I zonked out.

14

I dreamt of my grandmother while sleeping in that tent. The scenery was dark, but for a time I could feel the soft mattress, the flannel linens of my childhood bed, and could make out the general outline of my old bedroom back home. A shelf lined in action figures and picture books stood out across from the bed. I spied the trunk on the floor, lid sitting half-open for the mound of toys inside, and a thin, yellow light that shifted as though it were reflected through water came from the crack in the door, giving me just enough light to see by.

At the foot of my bed, taking a deep breath and sitting up to keep from nodding off, was my grandmother. Her grey, curly hair had been combed back after a shower, and the smell of her talcum-scented body wash came in strong—a scent I hadn't experienced in a long time. After her death I'd kept a half-used bottle of the stuff in my bedside table, and would sometimes take a whiff, just to remind myself of her. She turned to me, her features partially illuminated by the hall light, and spared me a little smile that said, "Go on, get some sleep."

I looked up at the ceiling, feeling—for the first time in many years—truly at peace. The softness of the covers, of my pillow, made me feel like I was sinking into a pile of feathers and my eyes began to grow heavy. Feeling my grandmother sitting at the end of my bed, near my feet, I felt secure. She hummed a soft tune, rocking very slightly as she repositioned herself.

Then, like a switch had been flipped, the scene changed and an ulcerating worry dropped into my gut. Eyes open, scaling the walls of my bedroom, looking over the rows of Teenage Mutant Ninja Turtles on the wall, I sensed there was something very wrong in the room, but I couldn't pinpoint it.

There was silence. The light from the hall continued to shift, but the color seemed to transition from gold to orange. Then red.

Yes, I could see it now. Looking to the door, which still sat ajar, the light pouring in from the other side was red.

There was a shifting at the foot of my bed as my grandmother went to stand up. I looked to her, wanted to ask her to stay, but I nearly bit down on my own tongue when I found someone else had taken her place. Bathed in shadow, save for an outline rendered in violent red, was an unfamiliar figure. A man, judging by his firm and imposing carriage. Broad shoulders were highlighted in red, and the barest hints of a face—stern and grey—were visible from where I lay.

My chest became host to a tremor as my heart began to thud violently and my lungs felt suddenly withered to husks. Clawing at the bedclothes, which felt scratchy now, and impossibly heavy, I stared up at the figure and mouthed a name.

Corvine.

The man standing in my room, looking down at me, was Dr. Corvine.

Where the first scene had seemed like nothing more than a happy, vivid memory, this second act convinced me that I was descending into a nightmare. The knowledge did nothing to help me break out of it, however. No amount of lucidity could shatter the illusion. I was a captive in my own head, forced to sit through whatever debauched fantasy my imagination wished to conjure up.

Staring down at me, obscured by darkness, Corvine's voice entered my head. It sounded just like it had on the tapes I'd listened to back at his cabin, as though his voice box had been replaced by a Sony Walkman. "*It is for good reason that men fear the dark. Our kind are transient, hopeless things. Things destined to live and die, leaving nary an echo in the yawning corridor of eons.*"

Beneath a floorboard in Corvine's cabin, I'd found a box full of tapes and papers. Among them had been a hand-written note—a rather dramatic and seemingly hopeless one. Corvine now stood before me, and recited it verbatim. The last lines were most striking, though, and lingered in the back of my mind even as wakefulness stole over me.

The door has been opened. It's already too late.

Was this simply a mad dream; the product of a mind overwhelmed by fatigue? Or had Corvine reached out to me from beyond to remind me of this message he'd left hidden in his cabin?

I snapped awake with a groan, sitting upright. I found myself in the tent, the plastic floor of the thing damp with my sweat. The material, a light blue color, was thin enough towards the front that I could see the moonlight—quite bright at this hour—shining through it. The movement of the trees gave the impression of flow and movement, similar to the light I'd seen in my dream.

Jake was snoring peacefully, and beside him was Jane, sitting exactly where I'd last seen her, with her head lolling to one side. She'd had it, was unable to remain awake any longer. So much for shift-sleeping.

I rummaged blindly through my bag for a bottle of water and chugged it, preparing to go back to sleep, when a new sign of movement outside the tent caught my eye. The bright moonlight shifted in such a way as to accommodate the shadow of a someone who presently made a silent advance towards the tent. There were no sounds of snapping twigs, of rusting leaves or grass—as the visitor paused before the front end of the tent and knelt down there was only dead silence.

Unnatural, impossible silence, as if the person outside the tent was weightless.

Every muscle in my body tensed and it took everything I had to reach over and nudge Jane with my foot. She came to immediately, blinking away her fatigue, and shot me hard glance. "What?" she sighed.

From outside, the front flap of the tent began to unzip. The silhouetted figure, jet black and rendered starkly against the light blue material, was trying to get inside.

JANE HAD her gun pointed directly at the shadow in the next moment. "W-Who's there? Hands off the tent, else I'm gonna shoot!"

The unzipping did not cease, didn't even slow.

As the front flap of the tent was half-undone and a pale,

white arm entered into view from behind it, Jane made good on her threat and fired two rounds.

The sound was deafening, causing me to reach up and clutch my ears—too little, too late. Jake lurched up immediately, taking a seated position, and looked about the tent confusedly as the two shots tore neat holes in the plastic flap. The shadow painted across it had moved in the moments before Jane had pulled the trigger, avoiding the attack, and was now out of sight. Urging me to unholster my weapon, Jane reached forward and gave the flap a hard jerk to the side, glancing out into the moonlit night.

The woods were pitch black, but the clearing we'd chosen to camp in was well-lit by the golden moon above. Despite this light, our visibility was hampered by the presence of a thick fog that had settled in during our brief sleep. The abundant moonlight, when viewed through the lens of this ever-shifting fog, became a disorienting glare. At the edge of the clearing, standing rigidly amidst the columnar trees and visible only for its aberrancy in the scene, was a figure with large, misshapen eyes every bit as dark as the night.

The Occupant.

It had come for us.

Jane left the tent, rifle in hand, and quickly stood up, taking aim. Like she'd been practicing for this encounter her entire life, she squinted through the backlit fog and took a shot.

It went wide.

Jake was the next one out of the tent, shoving me aside and nearly knocking Jane over as he rushed several feet ahead. "B-Babe! Is it... is it you?" Looking out at the trees and singling out the sinister figure with the cavernous eyes and Jack-o'-lantern hack-job mouth, he somehow found it in himself to smile. "It's me! It's Jake. Elizabeth," he called, extending a hand, "come back to me, babe! You can fight that thing off, I know it! Come back to me!"

I'd gone through a sappy "love can conquer all!" phase in my youth, but this sorry idiot really took the cake. I crawled out into the fog and stood at Jane's side, pointing my gun at the Occupant as though I really knew how to use it. "There's no sense in chatting with her," I told him. "She's not listening. The Elizabeth you know is gone, Jake."

I may as well have been talking to myself for all the good it did. Taking a few more steps, arms outstretched, he appealed to the entity once more. "I came for you, Elizabeth. Get rid of that thing, that monster, inside of you! Leave it behind and come to me—I'll protect you, babe. I won't let it find its way into you again. Just... just listen to the sound of my voice. Fight it. Try and fight it!"

The Occupant, taking a slow, sure step out of the woods, glared at him with what I could only guess was animal amusement. With the hollows of its face lit up by the brilliance of the fog, Elizabeth's new inhumanity became abundantly—and chillingly—clear. Though possessed of a human shape, Elizabeth was looking less human to me than ever before. Her stomach was distended like she'd stuffed herself with food to the point of bursting.

I knew what she'd been feasting on—or rather, *who*— and the sight of that engorged belly made me writhe with fright. Large snakes—pythons and anacondas—sometimes swallowed animals many times their size whole, digesting them over long periods. Let's just say that the snakes wore it better.

Those black, vacant eyes like two holes punched into plaster stared out at us, and a mouth, like a ragged hole cut through a white tablecloth, drooped open in a low laugh.

Her face was stained in blood from the eyes down, and her orange hair was matted with it, like she'd spent the day with her face buried in an oozing carcass. How Jake could face such a thing and make his embarrassing overtures was beyond me.

Jane stepped up to the plate, muttering as she took aim, "If Romeo wants to be the bait, then so be it." With zero hesitation, she unleashed two more rounds, both of them narrowly missing Jake, and nearly connecting with the Occupant, who suddenly tensed. Had it not been for the fog, I'm confident she'd have hit her mark. With the fog throwing off her sight the bullets had veered just shy, and could be heard to sink into trees.

That was the moment when all hell broke loose.

The Occupant, turning its head to an unnatural angle the way I'd seen mantises on nature documentaries do while eyeing prey, glared at Jane with enough venom to kill an elephant. At meeting that gaze, Jane felt herself overpowered even from a distance and lowered her weapon, quivering. In an instant the fight had gone from her and her mind was doubtless crowded with memories of what it had been like, years ago, when this very monstrosity had lived inside her. The more I stared out at the Occupant, shuddered at its hateful visage, the more I sensed something like recognition in its gaze. The thing was looking at her as if to say, "*I remember what your soul looks like.*"

But it didn't speak. Instead, it ran.

Straight at us.

Darting into the fog at a pace that would have been impossible for Elizabeth alone to reach, the Occupant came swinging, a muffled noise breaking from the hollows of its throat. It was the low, miserable wailing of the world beyond —the "voices of the dead". As though Elizabeth's insides formed the very borders of the underworld, the sounds of the dead rose up from within her—a murmur at first, and then a full-on flood. Tortured wails, anguished screams drawn from a thousand different mouths, poured out from within the Occupant's rough-cut maw and added weight to the already haze-laden air.

The Occupant was upon Jane before she could hope to aim her gun, leaving her with no option but to use the rifle as a club. Attempting to take a swing with the firearm, Jane reared back only to end up caught in the monstrosity's grasp. A white hand closed around her throat.

The rifle hit the ground with a *clack*.

Jane lost her balance and fell, but she didn't make it to the grass. Instead, she was lifted by the throat, held aloft so that her face was awash in moonlight.

That was when I made my move. I hadn't practiced for this, wasn't sure I'd do everything right. For a split second I thought of Jane, of what she'd told me. *Point and aim. Squeeze the trigger.* Raising the gun and taking the Occupant in my sights, I held my breath and, with no little hesitation, pulled the trigger.

The gun went off with a crack, and the resulting recoil sent a shockwave through my arm so that I nearly dropped it. For a time, I didn't even look to see if I'd hit my target; the tingling sensation reaching up to my shoulder, the deafening boom of the shot, the ringing in my ears all came together and slowed my perception.

My first shot, it turned out, did *not* hit the target. It might have, except that I'd aimed just a bit too high, missing by a hair's breadth. The Occupant was every bit as surprised—or enraged—as I was, and dropped Jane to the ground, where she curled into a coughing mass.

Now *I* was the one in its sights.

I felt a pull on my arm. It was Jake, dragging me away from the ghastly figure. "C-Come on! We have to run! We've gotta get out of here, man!"

I barely heard him as I stared into that misshapen alabaster face. My legs felt like toothpicks stuck in the earth; as if moving them too suddenly, or in the wrong way, might cause them to snap. When he pulled my arm a second time, it was all I could do to remain on my feet, and I fell into him, the gun hanging limply at my side. The longer the thing stared, the less I could feel my body. As though the Occupant were staring into my blood vessels, damming them up, a numbness washed over me, limb by limb.

The fog deepened, closing in around the Occupant in a dense, white knot. I couldn't hear—or see—Jane any longer and hoped she'd managed to escape while I'd been dazed. From the sky above—a clear, black sky alight with stars— came a sudden burst of rain. A downpour, borne of seemingly thin air, began to strike the very clearing in which we stood, and though I couldn't be sure, I suspected that it ranged no further.

I noticed it first as the drops crashed through the fog and struck the grass with a sizzle—the sound of a pot of water on the stove boiling over. It happened again and again, until the fog was burnt away and the foliage all around us began to wither. Tall grasses crumpled, the tent began to lose its shape, the soil bubbled and an unbearable steam began to rise. I felt drops on my head and neck, my arms.

The rain was scalding hot.

At the center of this downpour, untouched by the burning water, the demoniac thing stared at Jake and I as if daring us to come closer. With boiling rain leaving dime-sized burns wherever it met our bare flesh, we did no such thing, and instead doubled back, covering our heads with our hands and diving beneath the cover of nearby trees. In my periphery, I caught another figure stirring—Jane. She was shielding her face with one hand, and lunged from the direction of the tent with something clutched in the other. A large, fixed blade knife she'd packed in her bag.

Jane had intended to bury this knife in the specter's throat, but the clearing was fast becoming a cauldron of bubbling sludge and she slipped, sending the knife through the top of the Occupant's foot and temporarily staking it to the ground. The thing howled, thrashing like a fish out of water, and the rain suddenly ceased. Hands covered in burning mud and the edges of her face seared and red, Jane barked a single word at the two of us before reclaiming her knife.

"Run."

I don't know why I ran. I suppose that my animal instincts got the better of me and I just followed Jake, rushing into the dark woods, fleeing that steam-heavy clearing, delirious with fright. There was no telling whether Jane would manage to succeed against the thing on her own, or whether she'd survive the encounter. In retrospect, I wish I'd stayed behind to help her. But instead, Jake and I took off, sprinting into the dark woods without a flashlight, hearts jackhammering in our ears.

Maybe Jane had thought she could handle the Occupant alone. Maybe she'd been trying to protect us—to ensure our survival, and the survival of our mission—and had wanted us to live to fight another day. In the moment, I didn't stop to consider her reasoning, I just followed her directions. I ran like hell, and I didn't stop running until I hit a tree dead-on and knocked myself senseless. Speeding through the forest with no light, with no idea of the landscape that might lie ahead, was dangerous business. In my mad flight I'd accu-

mulated many bumps and scrapes on the trees, and knew
Jake was in a similar position. Scrambling back onto my
feet, I leaned against a tree and massaged my pulsing
temples. "J-Jake... how are you holding up?" I asked. "Did we
outrun it?"

He didn't answer.

Trying to catch my breath, my chest aching and my
knees wobbly, I leaned up against a tree and cleared my
throat. "Jake? Where are you, man?" Realizing I still had the
gun in my hand, I tucked it into the holster and waited for a
response.

A minute passed. My respirations and pulse slowed
enough for me to take in the sounds of my surroundings. It
was just as I'd feared though. There weren't any noises for
me to take in.

Only silence.

In running from the camp, Jake and I had been separated. Though we'd gone in the same general direction, once
robbed of moonlight we'd apparently taken different routes,
and at the pace we'd been going it was very possible that
we'd put some distance between us. Scanning the canopy
for some trace of moonlight, I tried to fight back the queasy
terror that now crept into me. "Jake?" I called out.

No reply.

I was alone—and lost—in the middle of the Michigan
woods.

Doing my best not to panic, I started walking again,
wanting to get as far away from the Occupant as possible.
Jake was a strong, fast guy, and had it not been for his
unfailing optimism in regards to the Occupant, then he'd
stand a great chance of surviving the night. Jane knew the
woods, was an experienced hiker, and yet we'd left her
behind to tangle with the specter on her own. She was

tough as nails and had been through a lot in life, but this time she may have bitten off more than she could chew. As for me, I didn't know a damn thing about survivalism. I spent my days sipping overpriced coffees, reading books and watching *films* about the great outdoors. I was out of my element. Shit, my element was in another universe completely.

I needed to keep moving. Though I felt confident that I'd escaped the Occupant for the time being, there was always the possibility that it would catch up to me. Woodland terrain and darkness were no hindrance to it, and it would descend on me without my even knowing it if I didn't start walking. If I could find a familiar landmark—perhaps the church we'd seen in Milsbourne—then I could take shelter and, when the time was right, find my way back to the camp, where I hoped to rendezvous with the others.

With this plan in mind, I took off through the trees, feeling my way through the black woods.

Now and then I paused to listen for signs of pursuit. Rustlings made by what I prayed were woodland animals sometimes sounded, but died out just as quickly. I heard a bird break the silence from some ways up, and the buzzing of insects wasn't hard to come by. Relieved that I'd managed to put some ground between myself and the Occupant, I quickened my pace and started up a slight incline, using trees to pull myself along.

What I didn't see coming, thanks to the pervasive darkness, was the drop-off.

I'd been marching along the top of a hill for some minutes when, stepping too far to the right, my foot slipped and—despite some attempts to ground myself—I began tumbling down an especially sharp incline. Hitting trees and rocks along the way, getting the wind knocked out of me, my hands shot out in different directions and tried to find an anchor I could take hold of. Gaining speed, I fell into a log-roll and felt something dense meet my head—a blow that immediately drew blood. Rolling a while longer, I was hardly conscious by the time I arrived at the bottom of the hill, and was left in a crumpled heap beside a cluster of fallen branches. My brow growing slick with blood, I struggled a few times to sit up before finally succumbing to the dizziness.

I was out like a light, and wasn't sure I'd ever wake again.

15

Once, at a college party, I'd gotten drunk. I mean, *really* drunk. One minute I'd been telling all my best jokes and wandering around my best friend's apartment with a fifth of cheap vodka, hip-thrusting to the music, and the next I'd been spewing all over his kitchen floor. I'd probably been on the verge of alcohol poisoning—that fifth of vodka merely the nightcap to a full day of drinking.

When I came to in the morning, I was still in my buddy's apartment, in his roommate's bed. A number of guys had carried my drunken ass inside, and when they'd been reasonably sure I wouldn't pull a Jimmy Hendrix, they left me there. Years later it made for a funny story, and it taught me not to underestimate the liquor, but there's always been an aspect to it that's unsettled me—the part where I awoke from my vodka coma.

Someone at that party had turned the air conditioner on full blast at some point in the night, so that the first thing I felt upon coming to was sheer cold. It was such a strange thing, coming around that morning. At first, I couldn't move —couldn't even open my eyes. My brain flicked back on like a computer doing a manual reboot, but I was, for at least a few minutes there, a complete vegetable. Then my thoughts kicked in, and my body's sense of temperature, too. *What's going on? What's happened to you?* I'd asked myself, heart suddenly racing. *Why's it so cold? Where are you?*

The cold had seeped into me throughout the entire night, making me feel like a specimen on a cooling slab. When my limbs finally thawed enough to move—and they took their damn time, believe me—I was able to sit up, my head still spinning, and get a look at the unfamiliar room. There was sunlight coming in through the window. Everyone else was still asleep, passed out in the other rooms. Minutes later, disturbed at the lengthy blank in my memory, I tried to piece together the night's events, to no avail. I stood up after a while, pinched myself. I probably did it four or five times over the course of that day.

Because, in some way, I'd felt like I'd died. My entire body, my brain, had shut down for the night, and when I'd come to, cold and confused, I'd felt like a revenant being drawn back into the world of the living. There was a small part of me—a part that still remains—that wondered whether I hadn't actually died on that bed, the night of the party. And there's a part of me, too, that wonders whether everything I've experienced since then has been a kind of dream.

Well, waking up in the woods with one motherfucker of a bump on my head and twigs in my hair after taking a plunge down the side of that hill was much the same. Awareness even returned to me in a similar fashion. There was the stiffness, the coolness like a blanket tucked around my limbs, the temporary inability to open my eyes. When they finally did snap open, I half-expected to see the inside of my friend's apartment.

Instead, I got a look at the thick, swaying canopy. There was a little moonlight peeking through. It was still nighttime. The Occupant would still be on the prowl, if Eli Lancaster was to be believed. The realization almost crushed me, though after all that had transpired I have to admit I didn't have much spirit left to lose anyhow, so I took a deep breath and took stock of myself.

By some miracle, my gun remained holstered. I gave it a pat, thankful to have a weapon, and then slowly stood up my battered frame so that I could examine the other resources at my disposal.

Surprise, surprise. I didn't have anything useful. There was a little money in my wallet, but I doubted I could slide a bear a few bucks for a couple of Aspirin. I had a lighter on me, but it was nearly spent. That was all. A flashlight, some food and clean water, would have been grand, but in my escape from the campsite I hadn't had time to gather up essentials.

Or any of Jane's goddamn cigarettes, for that matter. I swear, I'd have traded an icy bottle of Evian for a smoke just then.

My limbs pulsed angrily, and I could tell exactly where, in a few days, some truly eye-catching bruises were going to show up. Nothing seemed broken, though, and except for the soreness in my joints my body didn't seem too averse to walking.

I wondered how the others had fared, how many hours had passed since our encounter with the Occupant. Were they still alive? Were they safe? I felt a pang of guilt for leaving Jane behind, but it was soon overshadowed by my own desire to survive. At present, I needed to worry about numero uno. Internalizing this, I resisted the urge to call out to them—lest I get the Occupant's attention instead—and started walking, slowly.

There was still a lot of fog. It picked up the moonlight and amplified it in a peculiar way. While this did help to illuminate certain pockets of the woods, it gave a false sense of clarity from afar. Due to the fog, I couldn't accurately judge my location, and even clearings would be dangerous since I wouldn't be able to tell what I was heading into. My top priority was finding some safe place to stay the night— rather than covering a lot of ground. Running into these dark woods was stupid. I'd learned that the hard way. If I took another fall like the least one, it would probably kill me.

I paced on slowly, keeping my eyes peeled for structures in the woods. I wasn't sure what direction I'd fled in, or how close I was to the Milsbourne church, but if I could find it again then perhaps I'd be able to get back to our campsite. I tried studying the sky, searching for the black steeple, but the growth overhead was too thick.

Limping between trees, swatting at the occasional bug, I stepped out between a couple of conifers and spotted what looked to be a small shack in the distance. It was an encour-aging sight—if there was an old habitation out here, then perhaps I wasn't so far from the old mining town after all. I started towards it—excitedly at first, then with a halting caution—trying to gauge what sort of place it was, whether it was uninhabited.

I'd stepped within twenty feet of it when my intuition told me to back up. The leaning shack—an oversized shed by today's standards—was in hideous shape and looked as though it might topple into a pile of weathered toothpicks with the slightest nudge. The door was missing, and though it was hard to make out in the low light, I thought I could see a narrow window positioned beside it. It wasn't the structure itself that put me off. I'd seen a few of these already. It was the notion that something might be lurking inside, preparing to reach out of that open doorway or window to grab you as you wandered by.

There was something about that little window, in particular. A darkness *within*, or separate from, its darkness. Was the moon playing a trick on me, or had I seen something move in the window? I stared ahead, squinted, wondering if it was my imagination. If I focused hard I thought I could see something twisting and swaying in the darkness.

I took a couple of steps towards it, then wandered off to the side a little, then approached. This awkward dance brought me within a stone's throw of the little abode, and from this proximity, the moonlight more abundant for a thinning in the trees, I could see it in its entirety. It turned out there was nothing in the window except for a dangling knot of spider's silk, at the center of which rested what looked like a hummingbird.

Satisfied with my inspection of the shack, I left it behind me and pressed on in search of more. I chose my route based on what looked brightest, and followed the larger drifts of moonlit fog in the hopes that they might lead me to more open spaces, like those which might be found in the old town. And as I went, I thought back to the Occupant. It had shown up at our camp, just like Eli had claimed it would.

Thinking back to the incident at camp, I wondered what the Occupant's endgame was—if it had intended to split up our group so that it might poach us one by one. The thought was too horrifying to even entertain. Nothing the Occupant did made any sense to me, and not even Jane, who'd had a more intimate connection with it, could explain what its true motives were.

Stumbling over a large root in the fog, I cursed under my breath and had a look around. The moon was still high in the sky, bearing down on the forest. It was strange to think that elsewhere in the world, other people—oblivious to my plight—might look up at that same moon under very different circumstances—from their back yards or balconies, taking in the cool breeze.

Whether it was from the fog or from somewhere deeper in the woods, I couldn't say, but as I stood there I felt some-one's eyes pressing into me like a gun tucked into the small of my back. I must have looked like a baby rabbit sensing an oncoming hawk before it moved in, looking from side to side, pawing feebly at tree branches and fog to try and get a look at what my gut told me was coming. Someone was watching me intently, but I couldn't see them no matter where I looked.

Next came the noise. A low chorus of moans and wails emanating from the woods to my back, in the direction of the shack I'd just left behind. Like nails on a chalkboard the murmurings of the dead struck my ears and set me on edge. The Occupant was drawing near. I had no option but to keep moving, but I nevertheless faltered as I considered the futility in it. How long could I run? Wouldn't it be easier if I simply gave in, surrendered now? Throwing in the towel seemed perfectly pragmatic to me just then.

Thankfully, my survival instincts won out and, relying on what little juice I still had left in the tank, I started running again. I wasn't sure where I was going, couldn't see too well even when I came upon a pocket of moonlight, but

I prayed I'd get clear of the Occupant and find a good place to hide.

From behind me, the voices of the dead—streaming from within Elizabeth's body as though it were a loud-speaker—grew louder.

16

When I broke into a section of woods where two rows of crumbling wooden cabins stretched on into the distance, I wasn't sure whether it was a sign of good fortune or bad. Lungs burning and legs feeling like they might give out under me, I'd charged through the woods, heedless of any obstacles, and managed to escape, however temporarily, the cacophony issuing from the Occupant. The fog was heavy here, but not so heavy that I couldn't make out the dark, rough edges of a few dozen buildings. Some were completely broken down, mere heaps of lumber, but others had managed to endure. There was something like a road running between the rows of houses, long overgrown with grass, which I quickly started down. The years had blurred the lines—it had never been fully paved—but there were no tall trees here to block out the moon.

I beat it down the makeshift path, sparing the buildings brief glances as I jogged. Some still had doors to them. One, I couldn't believe, had an unbroken window. After I'd run past ten or fifteen of the things, I found them all to be of similar construction—basic and boxy. These, probably, had been homes to the many families who'd lived in Milsbourne prior to 1870. That any of them still survived was a marvel; that so damn many were still standing, I admit, creeped me out. The air of such a place was at once desolate and yet somehow crowded, for as I passed each and every of the dark cabins I felt as though their tenants had never really left, and were watching me from the windows.

Listening closely for any signs of the Occupant, I felt what was surely a premature rush of relief when only the sounds of my own frantic steps could be heard to echo against the worm-eaten buildings. Bounding down the grassy road, I looked more of the tenements up and down, wondering what they were like on the inside—if they weren't too unsafe to take shelter in, if they'd make good hiding spots. The road ahead seemed to slowly give way to more forest as I approached the end of the trail. I wasn't sure what awaited me beyond, but needed to stop somewhere and get my head straight. Better yet, if I could stay in one of these cabins till morning without encountering the Occupant, perhaps I could get some much-needed rest.

Stopping at the end of the road, eyeing the specimens closest to me, I chose the last one on my right side, a squat wooden box whose roof, by some miracle of frontier design, had not completely caved over the years. This one had a door, a solitary window, and looked to be somewhat spacious. The door was especially welcome, because if I could somehow secure it, I'd only have to worry about the Occupant coming in through the window. Sidling up to the cabin after taking one last look at the foggy expanse behind me, I drew my gun and approached the door. If there was a wolf or mountain lion using it for a den, I was about to evict it.

I reached out and eased the door open. The hinges weren't smooth in the least, sounded like they'd been completely rusted over since the Emancipation Proclamation, and the thick wooden door rumbled stubbornly against my hand as it opened. Pushing at it with my whole body weight, I managed to squeeze inside, where I took a tentative look around the dark room and waited for my eyes to adjust. A bit of fog had entered through the busted window, gathering about my feet and swirling in the corners. I blinked in the darkness, leaning against the door to shut it once more, and tried to get the lay of the land. There was a fallen chair in one corner, too rickety to sit in. A wood burning stove sat immediately to my left, surrounded in fallen twigs and leaves.

There was movement.

Towards the wall opposite the door, I spied a hunched figure. Only their feet were visible in the moonlight. Brown boots. I glimpsed a bit of tattered denim. I was about to approach, brandishing the firearm in clear sight. Before I could even utter, "Who's there?" they suddenly rushed towards me.

In my surprise, I dropped the gun. Rather than hit the trigger, I accidentally loosened my grip on it and it smashed loudly onto the sunken floors. Scurrying quickly towards me in a sort of wild crawl, the figure in the cabin made a desperate reach for the firearm.

17

Without thinking, I kicked the gun away—to a corner of the room where neither of us could hope to reach it quickly—and then delivered a swift kick, knocking the figure onto his side with a grunt. "Who the fuck are you?" I asked.

Coughing and attempting to right himself, the stranger wiped at his face and looked up at me. I pinned him to the floor with my foot, my heel digging into his chest, and then bent down to have a better look in the moonlight.

I recognized this face.

Stepping away and recovering my gun, I slid it into the holster and regarded the man—one of the guys who'd been paling around with Eli Lancaster—cooly. Unless I was mistaken, this man's name was Paul Coleman. He'd been the tight-lipped local that Jane had tried to ply with drinks at a local bar for information related to Milsbourne. It'd been this guy, too, who'd blabbed to Eli about the situation and had led him to Jane's trailer.

Paul had struck me as the cowardly type the first time I'd ever set eyes on him, and as I appraised him then, in the cabin, this impression was only reinforced. He looked up at me flinchingly, massaging his jaw where my shoe had caught him, and then he scampered back to his spot against the wall—slowly, as if injured—to bask in the darkness.

"It's Paul, isn't it?" I asked. "What the hell are you doing here?"

The man took a shuddering breath through his almost toothless mouth. The wispy whitish hair sprouting from his head looked like a wig of fog. He didn't say anything.

"You were with Eli Lancaster, right?" I took a step towards him, trying to look less threatening than before. "Sorry, I didn't mean to hurt you. I was actually hoping to take shelter in here."

Paul kneaded his hands in his lap. "It's following you, eh?" He cleared his throat. "You're a friend of Jane's?"

I nodded. "Yeah, but we got separated. And that thing, the Occupant... it's been busy. It killed Eli and a lot of his men. I'm surprised you're still alive," I said. "You might be the only one."

"It's because I ran," he blurted. "I didn't want to come here in the first place. We came to the woods last night shortly after we left Jane's place. Eli was real agitated after that, said we needed to come out into the woods to have a look at things. But once we made it here, into Milsbourne, that *thing* was waiting for us. And it tore us apart." His Adam's apple trembled as he spoke. "I saw it descend on us from the treetops like a spider. It was so silent, so slow-moving. And then it opened its mouth. Have you heard it? It sounds like it has a thousand men in its belly, all of them being tortured. The voices coming out of its mouth were..."

"I need to know," I said, interrupting his frightened reverie, "if there's some way out of the woods. Can you show me? I'm lost. Don't know my ass from a hole in the ground when it comes to navigating in the wild."

Paul shook his head, eyes closing as he sighed. "I know the woods all right, but I won't leave until it's daylight. And anyway, I'll never make it out on this ankle of mine." He grasped his pant leg and lifted his right leg up as though it were a dead limb, letting it drop to the floor. "I twisted it while I was running away from that thing last night... think I tore something. I stopped in here because it seemed like the safest place to rest and hide, but..." He whispered this next part, and I almost felt as though he were reading from a script of my own thoughts. "Ever since I've entered these woods, I've felt like I'm being watched. It's got eyes every-where, this thing. You can't escape it." He cradled himself, looked on the verge of crying.

"What happened last night? You say that you guys arrived in Milsbourne and she was waiting for you? Did she attack you outright, or did you provoke her?"

He gulped, apparently pained for the remembrance. "We made it into town, visited the old church. Eli's been a keeper of this place for most of his life, being a Lancaster and all. He said something didn't seem right... Well, it turns out he was right. That thing was waiting for us. It came down from a tree, dropped on us like an animal. And then it started to kill. Some of the guys were so scared they couldn't shoot. They tried running away, like I did. I was a lucky one, but some of those that got caught by the thing probably wished in their final moments they'd never been born at all. It literally broke a man in two, pulled his innards out like yolk of an egg. I saw it drink blood. I saw it eat parts of 'em, too." Tears spilled down his emaciated cheeks. "It's the devil, plain and simple."

I'd seen the gore scattered throughout the woods, so I

knew he was telling the truth. Horrified as the three of us had been to find the remains of Lancaster's men, it sounded like Paul's memories of the slaughter were even more night-marish. Nevertheless, now that I had this man to myself—someone who had claimed to know about Milsbourne's history, but who had been too tight-lipped to speak frankly with Jane in town—I steered the conversation in a different direction. "Jane approached you, wanted to know about Milsbourne. And Eli, before he died, mentioned a Lancaster curse. Now, I understand that you didn't want to talk before, but considering all that's happened, I hope you can give me some answers. I think that my friends and I are closer to solving this thing—and sending that monster back to Hell —than anyone in history. But I'm going to need your help. What can you tell me about all of this—about the town of Milsbourne, the creature out there, about the Lancaster family and the curse that Eli referred to?"

Paul, surprisingly, looked eager to talk. Maybe, consid-ering how close the specter of death had loomed over the past day, he wanted this to serve as his final confession. "I don't know what good it'll do now, but I'll tell you. I'll tell you everything. Someone ought to know, and if Eli's dead, then it may as well be you."

I looked to the window, choked with fog, and then stood near the door, arms crossed. "I'm all ears."

18

Paul began. I did my best not to interrupt him as he told his story.

"My ancestors came from Milsbourne, were amongst the first to settle there. Like most, the people of my line were miners. The Lancasters, too. Anyone with any kind of close family ties to Milsbourne knows all the stories about the Lancasters. That family's business is something that people have tried to put out of their minds for years, and yet they insist on passing it down generation to generation like some folktale. To hear my father tell it, it all started in the 1860's or thereabouts. The curse, that is.

"Back in those days there was a man by the name of Joseph Lancaster, a miner. Don't know much about his background, but I imagine he moved up to the UP—to Milsbourne—in search of a job like many others. And believe me, there wasn't no shortage of jobs at that time. The mining trade was booming. Well anyhow, this Joseph Lancaster nearly died one day when the shaft he was working in collapsed. This wasn't such an uncommon thing, mind you. Back in those days, when they didn't have access to modern equipment, miners died pretty often. Lots of 'em buried in these hills, as I understand it. Joseph should have been among them, but for whatever reason, he survived.

"When a man narrowly avoids death, there are always stories. But this was really something else, because everyone agreed that the man should've bought the farm after what happened to him. He was deep in the mines when the collapse occurred, was pretty well-buried. It should have been the end of him. The story goes that, while he was delirious and half-dead in the mineshaft, he made contact with something. Some devil that'd lived in the hills since the days of Creation. This thing offered him an out. It offered to save his life—and to give him and his line all the wealth in those hills—in exchange for one of his daughters.

"Evidently old Joseph took the devil up on his offer, because one day, after the townsfolk had already held a funeral for him and he'd been properly mourned, he comes walking back into town like nothing ever happened. Not a scratch on the sonofabitch. And people *talked*. Oh, they talked and talked. They welcomed him back, of course, acted happy to see him. But behind closed doors, everyone felt like something was wrong. A man ain't supposed to come back from an accident like that, and long before the truth came out people had their suspicions. Nice though they were to him when they saw him in town, the people of Milsbourne kind of gave him the side eye from then on, didn't trust him.

"Well, Joseph had a single child, a daughter, named Sarah. Sarah Lancaster was a nice, lovely girl, according to the stories. Probably a teenager, close to marrying age back in those days. Joseph, who no longer worked in the mines after his accident, started doing odd jobs to get by, which apparently gave him a lot of free time. It was then that a few people in town started noticing the trips he was making to the hills—for someone that wasn't working in 'em anymore, he sure was spending a lot of time there. Mostly at night. And mostly, they claimed, with his daughter in tow. Naturally, people asked a lot of questions. They weren't sure why he was doing it, and some people even decided to trail him, to spy on him.

"It would come out later that he was bringing her there, to the very shaft where he'd been buried, preparing her for some kind of big event. He called it the 'Communion of the Abyss', and it involved the two of them spending time near the mines on an almost nightly basis. This kept on for a little while. And then one day, the girl just up and vanished. Joseph acted concerned, plead ignorance, but those who knew about his little trips into the hills didn't believe him.

"Some eavesdroppers had theories. They thought he'd killed the girl, abandoned her in the mineshaft for some reason or another. Some claimed to have seen him fucking the girl—his own daughter—in the light of the moon, and there *were* murmurs from some of the womenfolk before Sarah vanished that she was with child.

"People were on edge after Sarah went missing, but they didn't *really* get the dots connected until others in town—mostly those who were close to Sarah, friends and loved ones—started disappearing, too. The girl's mother was the first. Then a childhood friend. Some others. All of them within the space of a week or two. And always disappearing by night.

"People got wise, managed to trace the disappearances to Joseph's strange behavior around the mines. A big group got together, and without telling Joseph, they set out for the mineshaft where he'd had his accident—left abandoned by the townies ever since the collapse—and discovered something wretched inside.

"They found the girl, Sarah, at the bottom of this mine shaft. Somehow, it'd been cleared, and when the sun or moon was right, you could see right to the very bottom. She was down there, her belly mighty round, and looked up at the townsfolk with black eyes. That wasn't all, though. The bodies of the missing people—her loved ones—were down there, too. Or, at least, what was left of them. She'd taken to eating them, drinking their blood.

"This caused a sensation. Story goes that they dragged Jospeh out of bed, brought him to the mine. The angry mob forced him to explain himself, and he spilled his guts right then and there. He told them all about the thing he'd met in the mineshaft—the thing which had since taken up residence in his daughter—and about how it had promised him his life, along with vast riches, in exchange. The townspeople were outraged and executed him on the spot. It's said they threw him into the pit, where he died on impact, and then dropped so much burning refuse into the shaft that they burned Sarah alive. People from town stood outside the shaft in shifts, keeping the fires going, until they knew for sure the girl was dead. That's how scared they were of her.

"But it didn't end there. Shortly after the girl's death, the water in town—clear and clean as anyone could ask for—started going bad. People ended up with a hideous bug, and those that didn't die were left severely disfigured. And one day, a clear one, if the stories are true, it began to rain. The rain was scaldingly hot, though, and people who got caught in it died excruciating deaths. This boiling hot rain took out most of the crops and livestock, too. They all knew why it was happening—it was revenge. The devil from the hills was striking back at them for their killing of the Lancaster girl.

"Milsbourne emptied out after that. It was too dangerous a place—desecrated. People left their homes, their jobs, and fanned out across the UP. Some went far away, others relocated to nearby towns. Those that remained were mostly there because they didn't have a choice. In the 1870's, stories began to come out of a terrible, black-eyed thing that sometimes wandered the woods at night. Future generations, like mine, would think of this as a kind of urban legend—Jersey Devil bullshit. But to the people alive at that time, it was true beyond doubt. They feared that the thing hadn't been killed when they'd burned the girl alive—that some aspect of it was still active out there —and so most of them ran away from it.

"You can imagine how difficult this made things for the survivors of that line. The Lancaster family was a big one, I guess, and even though they didn't have nothing to do with what Joseph had gotten involved with, they were shunned, if not outright murdered. People believed that, so long as that line kept on, the thing in the woods would never stop. It was stalking around, waiting to take hold of a female Lancaster, so it could resume its work. It was a tradition, honored even by some of the clergy in the area, to murder any female baby born to the Lancaster line as a precaution. This fell out of practice as the years passed and the Lancasters naturally moved away or dwindled. Some that moved away even took on other last names for fear that people from Milsbourne would come looking for them.

"Come to the present day, not a lot of folk live around here. Eli was the last Lancaster in this area that I knew of, and he was childless. He did have a kid sister, though, Ophelia, who had a kid of her own. I think it was a girl. Now,

Ophelia was kind of unstable. Poor girl had a lot of issues, and I guess hearing about the Lancaster curse all her life, she tried to kill herself numerous times—and even tried to kill her daughter at one point. A lot of people who live in the area these days don't know the full story, or else don't believe in it. But Eli and his sister Ophelia did. They stayed away from the woods for a long time, fearing that the wandering thing might take hold of her. And when Ophelia had a girl of her own, she panicked. Ophelia failed to kill her daughter, and I think someone in town reported her to the authorities, because the kid got taken away and no one ever heard about her again. Shortly after that, Ophelia killed herself.

"Some years prior to that, there was some nosy writer fella who came poking around. Or maybe he was a teacher or something. He showed up in town, asked the locals if they knew anything about Milsbourne, and offered to pay anyone who was willing to talk. He was curious, interested in local history, he said. Eli, who was hard up for cash at the time and thinking there was no harm in it, started telling this guy bits and pieces. The fella kept asking questions though, poking around, until he heard about the Lancaster curse, and he decided to look into it. Marched off into those woods all by himself one day, hoping to write a book about what he found. I'll never know why supposedly brilliant men insist on doing such dumb shit, but he did it. He went out, saw the town, the mineshaft for himself. And when he came back, he wasn't quite the same. He was scared shitless, talked about how he'd seen something moving down there, and how at night he'd felt himself being watched and followed.

"Everyone in town thought that was the last of him, but some time later he came back, really pushy like, and demanded to see Eli again. He wanted to meet everyone in Eli's family, and one night he made his intentions clear. He'd come back to kill every Lancaster he could find. The man was armed to the teeth, had a car full of guns and knives. Said that until every last Lancaster was dead, the thing in that mineshaft would linger on. He'd had nightmares about it ever since his first visit, had seen it everywhere he went. Eli found out about this, tried to talk him down, and then—because he had no choice—killed the man himself. He's buried out here somewhere, where no one will ever find him. The townsfolk backed him up, told authorities who came looking that the guy had gone hiking and never returned.

"I don't know what the thing really is—if it's really a devil and all that. After what I saw last night, I'd say that 'devil' is as good a name as any. You called it the 'Occupant'. Never heard that before. I'll confess that, until last night, I'd believed all of this was some kind of wild yarn. I'd been told these stories since I was a boy, but a part of me believed it was all just meant to keep me out of the woods at night. I'd never had reason to think on it too deeply. Not until last night. Eli, though, he believed. He'd always believed, to some degree. The older he got, the more stock he seemed to put into the whole thing.

"This awful thing is like an animal. It lives in the ground, eating its loved ones. It does that for nine months once it's been impregnated, and I imagine that, when it's gotten its fill, it sheds the host body like a snake and slithers out. I don't know how to stop the damn thing, but God help us if it ever manages to see it all through. I can't even imagine what that thing might look like once born... what it might do to this world. It would be the devil made flesh.

"This thing that Joseph Lancaster disturbed on that day

when he should have died has lingered in these woods ever since. People tried to send it back—priests, especially, have tried their hand at 'exorcising' it. Did no good. When they'd done all they could think of to send the monster back, the people of Milsbourne abandoned the town. It was the only path left to them. This thing should have stayed in the woods. It should have have wandered aimlessly until the end of days, when God Himself would be its judge. But somehow, Milsbourne's best-kept secret has come home to roost. It's real. All of it."

Paul looked tired, the words having left his parched lips a mile a minute.

Still standing near the door, I was left reeling by this new knowledge.

Suddenly, everything was much clearer.

This thing we called the Occupant was some kind of malignant spirit that had first been sighted in the 1860's, thanks to Joseph Lancaster. It should have been a wandering, impotent thing, relegated to the Michigan woods—and it would have been—if not for the work of Dr. W. R. Corvine. In the 1970's, mourning the loss of his wife and daughter, Corvine had invited his niece, Jane, to a cabin in the Hiawatha region to establish a link to supernatural forces. Desperate for results, his experiments began to degenerate into madness. It was only after abandoning all ethics and experimenting with untested drugs that his subject, Jane, had made contact with the only supernatural presence in the region. The Occupant, having wandered aimlessly for a century, was drawn to Jane and given a temporary refuge during the doctor's nightly sessions.

Jane, however, wasn't a Lancaster. She could not fulfill the promise that Jospeh Lancaster had made a hundred years prior. And so, abandoning Jane to a sanitarium, he set out looking for someone who could fill the role of host. Somewhere along the line, and probably due to a nudge from the Occupant, Corvine learned of Milsbourne, Michigan, found out about the Lancaster curse, and then started looking for a descendant of that doomed line. He struck gold when, taking on a post at Chaythe Asylum in the 80's, he was introduced to Enid Lancaster. Considering his renown as a physician, Corvine could have worked most anywhere he pleased. That he'd chosen an Ohio asylum where a descendant of the Lancaster line was admitted was no coincidence.

But Corvine didn't have all the answers. He'd done some research, tried to channel the Occupant into Enid and had reproduced, to some extent, the Communion of the Abyss, as Jospeh Lancaster had done. Jane maintained that Corvine may have impregnated the girl, and the general aesthetic of the sub-cellar chamber at Chaythe Asylum did call to mind the subterrane setting of the mineshaft in Milsbourne. Eventually, by experimenting on Enid's mind the way he'd done with Jane, Corvine created a perfect host for the Occupant.

Unbeknownst to him however, Corvine himself had been an unwitting host to the entity. Having been touched by death in his years, Corvine, who'd had contact with the Occupant at Hiawatha, had brought it back with him to Ohio when he began his experiments with Enid. Jane had stressed to me the Occupant's ability to act through all those who were touched by death—I myself had felt the thing's pull over my life, and had been utilized in similar fashion, to bring Elizabeth Morrissey to the asylum.

Corvine's experiments did not yield the expected result. The Third Ward Incident took place, resulting in multiple deaths. The doctor managed to strike his patient dead before she could escape, but knew its spirit would linger in the asylum, as it had done in the Michigan woods before he and Jane had disturbed it. Understanding the severity of the situation, Corvine had sprung Jane from the sanitarium and hoped to somehow channel the spirit afresh—to "close the door"—and send it back to wherever it had first come from. Jane, unwilling to be his guinea pig any longer, killed and buried him.

For decades, until Jake, Elizabeth and I became involved, the Occupant had wandered the shuttered Chaythe Asylum.

Just like W. R. Corvine, I'd been used to bring the Occupant into contact with a female Lancaster. Corvine had done so more or less knowingly. I hadn't known that I was being manipulated by forces outside myself until just recently however—my involvement had seemed like nothing but a strange coincidence. Had I known what was really going on, I never would have visited the asylum. I never would have gotten to know Elizabeth, or signed on to advise her damn club, for that matter.

During our exploration of the asylum, Elizabeth had gotten separated. Jake and I had found her in the sub-cellar chamber where Corvine had done his experiments—re-enacting the Communion of the Abyss—but what had happened to her in the interim was a mystery. It was clear to me now that the entity had made its move during that time, taking hold of her. I didn't understand the mechanism behind its possession. Elizabeth was a Lancaster, it turned out, and perhaps her interest in the supernatural had made her more open to possession. Her experience with death— caused by a murder attempt by her mother, Ophelia, while she was still living near Milsbourne—may have been the event that'd primed her as a vessel.

At some point, Elizabeth and Jake had had sex. Whether

it had occurred before or after the trip to the asylum, I was unsure. Whatever the case, that'd been the last piece of the puzzle, because upon my return from Hiawatha, I was informed by a battered and frightened Jake that the Occupant had taken hold and that Elizabeth was now missing. We tracked her all the way to northern Michigan, feeling all the while that we were being led.

And now, I realized beyond a shadow of a doubt, we had been. For a very clear purpose.

The Occupant had known we'd come looking for the girl. I, her trusted professor. Jake, her loving boyfriend. The entity intended to use the two of us as fuel for the body that now gestated within Elizabeth's womb. We were to be eaten by the girl, just as Sarah Lancaster's loved ones had been used for sustenance in the 1860's.

It all made sense. The lines were all connected.

And I felt more hopeless than ever before for this knowledge.

I was going to thank Paul for what he'd told me, and was thinking of other questions I might ask him, when the fog outside the window thinned and I glimpsed something in the corner of my eye.

There was someone standing outside the cabin.

And they were staring through the fog.

I tensed, immediately pulling my gun out. Paul flinched, backing against the wall. Nodding towards the window, my voice shriveling into a whisper, I said, "We have company."

19

The Occupant came in through the window, climbing in effortlessly and landing on the weathered floors with nary a sound. Backlit by the moon, its body wreathed in fog, it looked to the two of us in turn, as if trying to decide who to strike down first. Its face was so inhuman that its expressions defied easy description, and yet as it stared at us, mouth framed by rust—traces of its last meal—I thought I could make out something of amusement.

Paul screamed. Before the thing had entered, he'd been panting, trying to calm down after sharing all he knew. Now that the Occupant was inside, he loosed a terrible howl of fear and clamped his hand over his mouth, as though his retelling of Milsbourne history had somehow summoned it here. Despite the injury to his ankle—great terror often trumps great pain, in my experience—he stood and began hobbling towards me, his intention quite clear. He wanted to take the gun from me, or else use me as a shield.

The movement caught the Occupant's eye and it reached out, taking hold of Paul's shirt and dragging him close. With a pale hand wrapped around the back of his head, the occupant brought its drooping maw to his throat and bit deeply. Windpipe, crucial vessels and more were wrenched from his neck, and with a face dressed in gore, the Occupant turned to me with what I took for a crimson smile.

I fumbled with the door, tripped over my own feet as I sought to escape, and clumsily fired off two rounds, both of which ended up in the old cabin's exterior. Unwilling to watch the grotesque spectacle any longer and having no faith in my ability to fire a gun, I took off running as fast as my legs would carry me, sprinting back onto the main road between the rows of cabins and into the woods beyond.

It wasn't long before I hit what seemed to be an incline. The fog rolled by in thick waves, and the sparse trees on this fringe of Milsbourne made it easier to see. I was going up a hill, a very high and steep one by the looks of it. It was so steep in places that I had to crawl on hands and knees just to make it up to the top. When I did, I kept on running, sticking to the empty spaces where the moon was bright and pausing only, at the very top, to look back at the road I'd just left behind.

Striding calmly, confidently through the fog after me was the Occupant. It could have run after me, could have closed the gap between us without the least difficulty, but seemed to be enjoying the chase on some level. Like a persistence hunter tracking a prey animal, the Occupant was content to sit back and wait for me to tire myself out. Then, when my heart was on the verge of giving out and I'd grown optimistic enough to entertain the idea of survival, it would descend upon me. *Like a spider*, Paul had described it.

I kept racing, finding myself on a series of rolling hills. Some proved steep, others less so, but the burning in my quads made it difficult to continue at my breakneck pace.

Something was going to give if I didn't slow it down. Gritting my teeth, I scaled the summit of a real ball-buster of a hill and then started looking for a place to hide.

Mixed in among the trees were large outcroppings of rock. The terrain was changing; the farther I went in this direction, the rockier the scene became. Was I getting close to the old copper mines? Jogging down a gentle decline and peering into the fog-dense spaces between certain of the trees, I spied what looked like old mining equipment— primitive carts boasting large, rusted gears, piles of rusted chains and chunks of gnarled old wood that looked like they'd once been handles to shovels and picks. One of the geared apparatuses was rather large, and without thinking I raced around to its other side, dropping to the ground and pressing my back against it.

It was as good a hiding spot as any.

My breath was some time in returning to me. I looked down at my gun and wondered how many bullets I had left. I gave it a shake as though I'd somehow be able to hear them, and wiped the sweat from my brow. *Doesn't matter how many bullets are left if you don't start hitting something with them*, I thought. How differently things might've gone for me if only I'd spent a few days at a firing range, practicing. Jane's crash course had kept me from shooting myself in the foot, but I was hardly a marksman.

My body craved water and food. I realized I hadn't had a drink since leaving camp, and suddenly my mouth was feeling dry as a cotton ball. For most of the night I'd been running almost non-stop, and if I wasn't careful, dehydration was a real possibility. I hoped to encounter some source of clean water and, recalling the well we'd seen on our walk into Milsbourne, I wondered if it would be safe to drink from. But then Paul's story came to mind and I nixed the idea. He'd told me the water in Milsbourne had gone bad due to the Occupant's meddling. I wasn't sure if that was still the case, but didn't want to end up drinking any dangerous pathogens. My only hope for clean water was to get back to camp.

I was dreaming of guzzling a gallon jug of water and smashing a whole box of granola bars back at the tent when I heard a voice from up above. It damn near stopped my heart.

Sinister and smooth, the androgynous voice slipped into my ear and chilled my bones. *"I've had my eye on you for so long."*

Though my body protested violently, my eyes were drawn upward, to the pale, orange-haired figure that hung above me, suspended on the branch of a tree like a bat in a cave. Drops of blood from its stub of a chin struck the ground like red rain, and I felt some strike my arm. The thing leered, a low laugh oozing from its depths. The chorus of the dead was welling up again, streaming from the specter's eyes and mouth.

I was cemented to the ground, my legs fried by equal parts fatigue and fear. The air in my lungs just sat there, a check my body couldn't cash, and I felt the color drain from my face.

The Occupant touched down on the ground with other-worldly grace, slipping from the branch and arriving at my feet in a neat crouch. It was upon me in the next instant, its movements so fast and fluid that my feeble eyes couldn't keep up. It seized me by the shoulders with the force of ten men and brought its face up next to mine. I could hear the voices issuing from within its body, could smell something emanating from it, too—a mix of sulphur and sun-warmed carrion.

Its mouth fell open and a long tongue parted my lips, probing the inside of my mouth, my teeth, and slipping some ways down my throat, where it wriggled like a worm. It was the most repellant thing I'd ever experienced. Gagging on the thing's tongue, tasting traces of Paul's blood as its ragged lips pressed mine, I wished I was dead. The Occupant would soon consume me, would unhinge its jaw and swallow me head-first like some Amazonian snake, and it was just as well.

It pulled away, and I gasped in a deep breath.

"*I can taste your fear,*" it said, its black eyes widening ever so slightly. "*I'm going to kill you now, Stephen.*"

Though the feeling was gone from my body and I was wreaked with disgust, my right hand brought the gun to the Occupant's abdomen and my finger set upon the trigger.

The specter was amused, laughed as if to say, "*You haven't got the balls to kill your student.*"

I drowned out its laughter with a gunshot.

The bullet slammed into the Occupant's waist, and suddenly the thing was scrambling away from me, clutching at the new wound. A shrill scream pierced the night air, but it sounded less distorted than any of its previous vocalizations. It sounded almost human.

It sounded like Elizabeth.

Falling onto its back and squirming, the figure thrashed and howled. I stood up, pointing the gun at it once more and watching—with no little horror—as the thing's monstrous visage morphed into something more familiar. The black eyes were gone, and the mouth shrank back into its proper proportion. I was staring down at Elizabeth Morrissey.

I couldn't explain it. I'd gotten a good shot in, but was unsure why the Occupant's sway over Elizabeth should have waned after the blow. Elizabeth's eyes sprang open, full of tears, and then promptly rolled into the back of her head. She sucked in air between sharp cries of pain and clawed at the grass.

"Elizabeth!" I said, kneeling beside her. "Elizabeth, it's me!"

She looked in my direction, but there was little recognizance in her eyes. She was a creature fully consumed by her pain, and I got the impression that her mind was somewhere else, battling for dominion against the dark thing that'd been present until just moments ago. I looked at the wound, feeling a tsunami of guilt. Studying it more closely, it didn't appear to be a mortal wound—I'd gotten her in the side but had probably—hopefully—missed her vital organs.

I was considering how best to help her up, how to get her moved back to camp, when she fell silent and suddenly lurched upward. The wound poured blood down her leg as she rose—*levitated*—to her feet, and her mouth opened wide to loose the bloodcurdling screams of the tortured dead. A black eye sized me up, then another, and before I knew it I was staring the Occupant in the face once again. The thing struck me in the gut with a wild swing, knocking the air out of me, and then made a mad dash for the woods, clutching its side. The figure had disappeared into the fog by the time I looked up, and the sounds of its flight evaporated soon thereafter.

Shaking, I holstered my weapon and slowly stood up, the world spinning around me.

I was still alive, somehow.

And Elizabeth was still in there.

20

I wandered the forest, exploring the rolling hills and the edges of the mines. In my dazed state I had no business going anywhere near abandoned mine shafts, but found myself in the vicinity of not a few as I tried to find my way to civilization.

There wasn't any place in particular I wanted to go. I just wanted out of this mess entirely. Returning to camp would have suited me just fine, and I'd have quenched my thirst and hunger, happily reclining in the remains of the tent while awaiting my ultimate fate. A road or public camping area, too, would have been a welcome sight, and I wondered whether I wouldn't be able to spot one in the distance if I climbed to the tops of the highest hills.

My thoughts were dominated by two things: my unrelenting thirst and Elizabeth.

I solved the first problem when I came across a clear-looking puddle in a mossy divot of land and damn near drained it. Falling to my knees, I sucked up the water like a horse at a watering hole and almost wept as it flowed down my throat. I didn't mind the grit, the sediment, but drank deeply till I no longer felt like a dried-out husk inside.

The Elizabeth problem would not be easily solved, however.

Let me be perfectly clear: After everything I'd witnessed, after all the challenges I'd faced, I no longer had any problem with the idea of killing Elizabeth Morrissey. That isn't to say the act wouldn't haunt me for the rest of my days, or that it wouldn't instill in me great sadness. It would. However, at this point, I saw it for what it was: A necessity. Killing Elizabeth was probably not optional, despite Jake's wishes to the contrary. If the kid was even still alive, I hoped he'd been through enough to convince him. He'd been stubborn for too long, entertaining peaceful means of dealing with the Occupant. I was ashamed to have followed along for so long. Putting down Elizabeth was likely our only way out of this.

But then, killing her would only get us so far.

The townspeople of Milsbourne had burnt an Occupant-possessed Sarah Lancaster to death at the bottom of a mineshaft, but that hadn't been enough to return the spirit to the hovel it'd initially crawled out from. The spirit had gone on haunting the Michigan woods for a hundred years, impotent without a Lancaster to latch onto, but present nevertheless. It had done the same at Chaythe Asylum, lingering in its halls long after Enid Lancaster had been struck down.

Killing Elizabeth would get us out of immediate trouble, but so long as the Occupant walked the Earth—and the Lancasters did as well—it would always pose a threat. Though murdering every descendant of Joseph Lancaster might very well send the Occupant back to Hell, I doubted that it was possible to do so. His descendants had fanned out, possibly across the State—the country—and would be damn near impossible to trace. Never mind the serious problem I had with mowing down perfect strangers just because they shared a common last name.

There was something else bugging me, too. When I'd shot the Occupant the night before, I'd gotten a glimpse of Elizabeth. Somehow, she was still in there; her mind hadn't been totally squashed by the invading presence. I didn't have enough information to be sure, but I suspected there might be a way to oust the Occupant whilst simultaneously sparing Elizabeth. Dr. Corvine had evidently thought so— upon springing Jane from the sanitarium in '89, he'd set his sights on somehow sending the entity back to the shadows, and was looking to use Jane to do it. I wasn't sure of his plans—whether he had any reason to believe such a solution existed to the Occupant problem—but the possibility of a peaceful resolution, though far-fetched, intrigued and enticed me. I'd had enough of bloodshed, of senseless killing. I'd have loved nothing more than to return to my old life, with my students in tow.

I wasn't sure what day it was anymore. Making it back to Moorlake in time for the start of the semester was pretty much out of the question. If I survived this at all, I was going to be cashing in some serious sick days—consequences be damned.

The woods were so much easier to navigate during the day, I looked up and pleaded with the sun to stay out forevermore. It's possible, too, that I was talking to the sun because I was hallucinating, but a part of me was just happy to be able to see where I was going. Eventually, I was going to find something—our campsite, a familiar Milsbourne landmark, a paved road—and things would improve. I kept telling myself that, and even fed myself the lie that Jake and Jane were still out there somewhere, probably safe and sound, when in all likelihood their carcasses had probably been pulled apart like boiled chicken and their intestines had been strung up like Christmas garland.

There was a large, craggy outcropping ahead, and as I drew near I made out what appeared to be another mineshaft. I sidled up to it, taking a breather, and had a look inside. The sun rendered the opening in harsh light and gave me a decent idea of its total depth. A fall into such a thing would kill a man, easy. I stared down into the pit, giving my tired feet a rest, and then spied something white and brittle jutting out from some crag. I shouldn't have thought anything of it—it was likely an abandoned pickaxe, or some feature of the rock, but the longer I stared at it the more interesting it became to my fevered mind.

It was a bone.

I blinked, knelt down, and looked at it more closely. It was well out of reach, but I felt certain of it. It was a bone. Human, judging by the size.

I looked deeper down and discovered a couple more. Some were shaped like ribs. Further below, the round tops of what appeared to be skulls sat aglow in the morning sun.

This mineshaft was full of bones.

My heart skipped a beat as I stared down into the aperture, realizing where I was. There were loads of bones in this shaft—bones that had been weathered by the elements for a very long time. This, then, was the spot where Joseph Lancaster had had his near-death experience, and where his daughter had been burned alive for her sins.

Something shifted below, and I nearly pitched forward into the hole.

A pale, disordered face turned to meet mine from the

bottom of the chasm, and a wan hand beckoned me to hop in.

The Occupant.

By day it lives in the Earth. That was what Eli had said.

I didn't waste a moment. The sight of the bone pit inspired in me some lucidity I hadn't known I possessed and I was soon running full-tilt away from the mineshaft. I started down a hill, my heels sliding down the steeper parts and leaving deep ruts in the soil. It was then, as I burst through a copse of trees, that I entered into some familiar territory by sheer, merciful chance. A primitive road opened up before me and two rows of shabby cabins lined it on both sides. I'd been here the night before, had been chased here by the Occupant. I eyed the cabin I'd taken refuge in and felt a chill wander down my spine as I realized Paul's body was probably still inside. I had no interest in finding out what the Occupant had done to him after I'd left, and I put the cabin behind me, taking the road in the opposite direction, away from the hills.

An hour's walk through medium growth led me to still more promising scenery. The path I was on, which was punctuated with fewer trees than I'd expected, had probably been a long trail once used by the townsfolk. It was an hour's walk down this path before I spied the black spire of the church rising above the trees in the distance, but prior to that lovely sight I'd glimpsed a number of squat, tottering shacks and a collapsed well that solidified the feeling in my gut. *You're going the right way!*

The sight of the church really put some spring in my step, and after a short jog, I found myself standing outside it. The gore still remained in place, though the local fauna had seemingly gotten to the most conspicuous bits. Shoving the carnage out of mind, I stopped in front of the church and tried to gauge the direction of our camp. I wasn't sure what state I'd find it in, or if the others would be there, but I had to find it. Stepping into the dense woods, keeping my eyes peeled, I trudged on in search of the clearing we'd chosen and hoped that the blue tent would give it away from afar.

The tent, eventually, entered into view. It had been damaged severely by the boiling downpour the night before, but still remained standing. I ran towards it, my eyes crowded with tears, and burst into the clearing with a cry of joy on my lips. The site was still a mess, but I found some evidences of a fire that—judging from the warmth still issuing from the mass of spent wood—had been put out only recently. Had Jane or Jake started the fire? Were they still alive?

Hope really does spring eternal. I'd witnessed unutterable evil in these woods, but still held out hope that my companions had survived. The tent shook a bit as someone within moved to exit. I placed a hand against my holster and prepared to draw the weapon if necessary. "Who's there?" I asked in a tremulous whisper.

21

To my surprise—and delight—both Jane and Jake crawled out of the tent to meet me.

The way they looked at me you'd have thought I was Elvis Presley.

"Professor?" blurted Jake, his black eye still prominent on his face and his arms scored in burns for the previous night's rain. "Is it really you?"

Jane's welcome had been less warm. She'd come out of the tent with her rifle in hand, but at verifying my identity had set it aside. "Well, I'll be damned."

Because I surely looked like hell and was awfully unstable, they helped me into the tent and offered me food and water. The water from the gallon jug tasted a whole lot better than the puddle shit I'd swilled, and even after slamming four granola bars my stomach felt like a bottomless pit. I reclined, stretching out and allowing my pulsating limbs to relax. My heart was racing, but for once, it wasn't out of fear or fatigue. I was overjoyed to be reunited with the two of them.

Being separated from the group, forced to face the

horrors of the Occupant on my own, had been unbearable for me. I thought to tell them about everything I'd learned, everything I'd experienced, but before I knew it I'd fallen fast asleep.

Well, more like a coma.

They were good sports about it and let me sleep until the early evening. Frankly, unless they'd planned to carry me on their backs, or else abandon me in the tent, they had no choice but to let me rest. I was in terrible shape and wouldn't have been able to make it out of the woods without passing out on the trail. Jane roused me with a gentle nudge as the sun was beginning to dip in the sky. "OK, professor," she said, peering down at me. "Can't wait much longer. Get your ass up."

I looked up at her with heavy eyes, not sure if I was awake or dreaming, dead or alive. "What's up?"

Jake leaned over me, too. "What happened to you last night?"

My sleep had been dark and sterile. My brain had been too busy patching things up to dwell on the night's events, to waste time on dreams, but as I sat up in the tent, the memories came rushing back and with them came the concomitant terror. A question like, "What happened to you last night?" was not one that I'd be able to answer concisely. Gulping down some water, I sighed. "It's a long story."

I HYDRATED and took it from the top. I told them about how I'd gotten lost while running from the Occupant, and how I'd tumbled down a steep incline and hit my head. I described my wanderings through town—the old buildings I'd seen and my encounter with Paul. They were both surprised to hear that anyone from Eli's party had survived, and they listened closely as I unpacked the details of my talk with him. Recounting everything he'd told me about the history of Milsbourne, the Lancaster family and the fate of Jamieson Monroe, I saw the lights come on in their heads as they put the pieces together. After that, I described my hours of wandering in the hills, where I'd stumbled upon the mineshaft where Sarah Lancaster had been burned to death, and my eventual return to the campsite.

Jane, her gun never far, lit me a cigarette and reclined in the tent, deep in thought. "The Occupant was inside the pit this morning?" she asked.

I nodded. "Yeah. I looked down into it. The sun was just right, and I could see her waiting down there, probably nursing the wound I'd dealt it. I was so terrified I started running."

She grumbled, taking a puff from her cigarette. "That's a missed opportunity. You should have done something. You could have burned her alive—tried shooting her from up above."

I couldn't help but roll my eyes at that. It was possible that I could have killed the Occupant by taking potshots from the top of the aperture, but most every other shot I'd taken in my brief history as a gunslinger had been complete shit. More likely, I'd have simply used up my bullets and missed every time. And as much as I'd have liked to burn her the way the people of Milsbourne had done in the 1800's, it hadn't crossed my mind to try. Except for a crappy, spent Bic lighter, I'd had nothing to start a fire with.

There was also one other reason I'd given into my impulse to flee and hadn't attempted to put the monster down.

I held out hope of one final alternative.

Jake was listening carefully, and I saw him wince every time there was mention of hurting the Occupant. When I'd gotten to the point in my story where I described shooting her in the abdomen, he'd fallen completely silent. Learning moments later that the shot hadn't done the creature in, the idiot actually seemed relieved. Looking to stamp out this merciful mindset he was still holding onto once and for all, I pointed at him with my cigarette. "Now, don't get carried away with this, but something strange happened when I shot her. The bullet hit her, she doubled back, and suddenly she was Elizabeth again. Her face changed back, and her voice did, too. It was like I'd temporarily knocked the spirit out of her, made Elizabeth's body less hospitable to it. The change didn't last. The Occupant returned and she skittered away like a wounded animal, but I thought it was strange. It makes me wonder if maybe... just maybe... there isn't some non-lethal way out of this."

Jane looked at me with contempt, shaking her head and putting out her cigarette. "You really that soft in the head? After all you've seen, after all that's happened to your sorry ass, you still want to spare the goddamn thing?" She made a noise like a laugh, but was too disgusted for actual amusement. "That's ridiculous."

"What's ridiculous about it?" asked Jake. "If it's possible for us to save her, then we should absolutely try. The professor and I didn't come out here to become killers."

Jane cocked her head to the side. "Then the two of you shouldn't have come out here at all."

"Listen," I continued, "I know it's a stretch, but I'm not the only one who thought it might be possible to pry the Occupant out of its host. Remember your uncle? When he came back to the sanitarium, after the Third Ward Incident, he was interested in finding a way to send the Occupant back to the darkness, right? He wanted to use you in new experiments so that he could 'close the door', so to speak. What was he planning? How would that have worked?"

Jane stood up, stepping out of the tent and pacing across the clearing with her arms crossed. "Don't bring my uncle into this," she spat.

I followed her out. "But surely he had some kind of plan! Some experiment he'd hoped to try! Whatever it is, maybe we can recreate it and get rid of the Occupant for good."

She stared out into the woods, refusing to look me in the face. "You had all of my uncle's research," she said, shrugging. "Might have been something in there."

"There wasn't. And it's all gone, anyhow. You're the only lead we've got," I insisted. "When he came back and sprung you out of that madhouse, what was he planning? He had to have said something to you, given you an idea of what you could expect, else you wouldn't have killed him."

This caused her to turn, and the look in her eyes was hardly less hateful than that of the Occupant.

"Is he wrong?" asked Jake, arriving beside me.

Jane took her sweet time in responding, hands buried in her pockets and eyes riveted to the dimming sky. "It'll be night soon," she muttered, tonguing her molars. Finally, she delivered the goods, though not without her fair share of disclaimers. "It would never work. And he didn't explain it to me, not fully. I wanted no part of it. After what he'd put me through at the cabin I didn't even want to see him again. I'd wished he was dead long before I ever pulled the trigger. But when he came back, he finally realized that the Occupant was bad news—not to be messed with—and yes, he wanted to do experiments with me so that he could find a way to send it back to... Hell, I guess. To the shadows, where it came from.

"That would involve calling it back from the asylum, though. He knew it was still in this world, that it would wander the building where its last host had died. But maybe, he theorized, by letting it back inside of me, he could keep it there—contain it—until he found some way to get rid of it permanently. Like I said, I wanted no part of that. Wouldn't stand for it, and told him as much. If he wanted to use someone else as a guinea pig, then that was fine, but I wouldn't take part. Always a stubborn man, he wouldn't take no for an answer, though. He brought me back to that cabin and started preparing—doing lots of reading and shit. That's when I took action. I knew that if I didn't, his experiments would have me suffering through more of the same horrors. I knew that the Occupant would be back, and I was scared to death that it wouldn't leave this time. It hadn't liked me very much as a host—it had preferred the Lancaster girl at the asylum—but he felt confident he could invite it into me and then, when he had it in his sights, he'd try any number of things to destroy it. But what kind of sense does that make? It's like infecting your patient with a deadly virus and strapping her down in the hopes that you can find a cure before it eats her brain. It's madness.

"So, I shot him. The Occupant was far away, and as far as I was concerned, the nightmare was mostly over. I'd never forget what he put me through, but as long as I never had to experience it again, I told myself I didn't care, that someday I'd get over it."

The wheels started turning and I tried my hand at devising an experiment. When faced with a traumatic injury, the Occupant's sway over its host momentarily weakened. What if we could somehow make Elizabeth a less hospitable host for the entity by exploiting that? What if, through the use of limited—non-lethal—violence, we could push the Occupant out of her, allow it to temporarily take up residence in Jane, who'd be waiting nearby, and then abandon the dark spirit to the woods? I wasn't sure if it would work, but the fact that we could mess with the Occupant's connection to Elizabeth at all was too good a lead to overlook. If there was any way to get through this mess and let the girl live, then this was it.

I told Jane what was on my mind, and kept speaking even as she scoffed and scowled. "I need your help, Jane. I want to capture the Occupant. It'll be tough, but if we manage to shoot the thing—and you're a much better shot than I—then we'll find ourselves with enough time to bind her. We brought rope, right? Well, after that, like some witch-finder of Salem, we'll torture her a little—just enough to keep the Occupant from re-entering her, and when the thing has had enough, maybe we can get it to enter you for a bit. Hear me out—if the Occupant enters your body, it'll cause you great fright and discomfort, however it won't be able to establish a strong enough connection with you to harm us. Right? It needs a Lancaster to make that sort of strong connection. Jake and I can leave with Elizabeth, try to make it out of the woods, and when the Occupant has left you, like it always did during your uncle's experiments, then it'll be forced to wander the woods again and you'll be free to hike out of the forest as well."

Jake agreed enthusiastically to this, and even came up with an idea for baiting the spirit. "The two of you, with your guns, can hide nearby while I call out to her. When she hears my voice, she'll come closer and you two will have a great opportunity to wound her. Then we'll tie her up and do what the professor said. I think it might work!"

"Do you have any idea what you're asking of me?"

barked Jane. Though I could have been mistaken, I thought I saw tears in her eyes. "Do you know how long I've dealt with this? How long I've tried to bury the memories? And now you want me to... to let it in again, just like my uncle!" The way she looked at me just then, I feared she was going to blow my brains out, like she'd done to Corvine.

"Jane, I know I'm asking a lot," I replied. "And there's no way for me to know what you went through. But I'm begging you to consider it. Imagine what Elizabeth's going through right now."

She shook her head fervently. "That poor girl was damned from the day she was born. Her line, her blood, was cursed."

"Exactly. And from where I'm standing, this is the only way we can possibly save her." I stepped towards her. "Please. Help us save this girl, Jane. She's young. She's been through a lot, but she still has her whole life ahead of her. If this doesn't work, then we'll... we'll do the nuclear option. Kill her, dump her in the mineshaft like they did to Sarah Lancaster. Burn the body, too, if you like. Whatever it takes. But before we resort to that, let's try and save her."

Jane fumed at the edge of the clearing, muttering to herself. "And if it doesn't work?" she demanded. "If it all amounts to nothing?"

"Like I said, if it doesn't work, then we go with the original plan and kill her," I said.

She shook her head. "No. If it doesn't work, if things go sour, are you going to be able to live with yourself?"

I nodded. If I did everything in my power to bring Elizabeth back home, then I could die with a—mostly—clean conscience. "This is the path I want to take. I can't force you, but I'm begging you, Jane."

She looked to Jake, and then back to me, chuckling

darkly. "Guess I've been out-voted, huh?" She put her hands on her hips and returned to the tent. "I'll tell you what, I'm going to try this little experiment. Every nerve in my body is screaming right now, telling me not to. But I'll do it. If it's possible to spare this girl's life, it's worth a try. But if it doesn't work out, I'm not going to hesitate—or ask permission—to put a slug in her brain. Do you both understand me?"

I agreed with this. Jake, too, eventually agreed.

Now that we had a plan—and little remaining sunlight —we began to make our preparations.

22

W e chose the tottering church as the stage for our impromptu capture.

Though lacking confidence in the plan and running mostly on hope, I tried to keep spirits high as we packed the bulk of our things and began hauling them down to the church. We abandoned the tent and packed a particular bag full of the rope we'd brought for easy access. By the time we'd hiked to our location the sun had dipped past the horizon and was falling fast. Jane and I kept our guns close at hand and paced around the inside of the church, which was still done up in the Occupant's grisly décor, and which still boasted the body of Eli Lancaster up near the altar. Meanwhile, Jake stared out the door at the darkening woods and talked quietly to himself, rehearsing lines like a nervous kid in a high school play.

The plan was roughly this: Jake would wander a little ways from the church and call out to the Occupant, luring it with his voice. When it finally moved in on him, Jane and I would make our way outside to a strategic position to the right of the church, where we could probably manage clear

shots at the specter. We'd agreed not to aim for her vitals—
to try and hit her in the leg, arm, or some other place that
would induce the stunning effect I'd described—but Jane
couldn't fight back her smirk, as if to say, "Whatever
happens, happens." Finally, once the Occupant had been
wounded, the two of us would rush over to the temporarily-
freed Elizabeth and tie her hands and legs tightly. After-
wards, she'd be brought to the church, where we'd carry out
the transference experiment.

Seeing as how we were the only three things in the
entire forest that the Occupant had any interest in, I felt
confident that it would come. What would happen once it
showed itself, however, was anyone's guess. Corvine had
never tried something like this. His entire study into the
Occupant had been focused on giving the entity whatever it
wanted in the hopes that it would reward him. We were
breaking new ground, and I'd be lying if I said I wasn't
curious as to how it would play out.

When night was fully upon us and we'd run through a
few drills, Jane and I took our places within the church,
each of us standing to one side of the door with our guns at
the ready, while Jake began calling out.

"Elizabeth!" he cried. "Are you out there? Babe, it's me! I
want to see you. Are you out there?"

It was early yet, but a light fog was beginning to swirl
between the trees. I hoped it wouldn't interfere with our aim
when the time came.

"Elizabeth!" continued Jake. "It's me! Follow the sound
of my voice!"

Minutes passed and my faith in the plan wavered. The
Occupant was out there, somewhere, but what if it had
found us out, somehow? Could it smell this setup? For that
matter, what if the gunshot wound I'd left it with had

rendered it immobile for a time? Would it spend the night in the bottom of that mineshaft, resting?

Jake's voice wavered. "T-There you are," he said. "I've b-been looking all over for you."

Jane shot me a look. It was nearly time.

I tensed, wanting to rush out and start firing, but Jane, sensing this, shook her head. She'd give me the signal when it was time, and she edged narrowly towards the door to take a look outside. Gaze narrowing, she held her rifle close and watched Jake make his rehearsed overtures.

I peeked, too, and felt my heart pause as I did so.

The Occupant was standing within the treeline, looking at Jake intently. The breeze sent its orange hair swaying. It took a few slow steps out of the woods, practically gliding towards him, and as it advanced I could sense no difficulty or pain in its movements. It was possible—though I couldn't tell you how—that the wound I'd given it had healed up over the course of the day.

When the Occupant had come within just a few paces of Jake, and he looked so white in the face that I thought he might faint, Jane gave a firm nod. Rushing out of the church, bounding through the grass some ten or fifteen feet, she halted, raised the rifle and took aim, squeezing out two shots back to back. Without even waiting to see if those had connected, she moved slightly to the right and fired another pair. It was fluid, almost beautiful to watch.

I followed her out, holding the gun out before me and trying to size up the Occupant before taking a shot of my own, but by the time I thought to pull the trigger, the thing had already fallen to the ground in a heap.

Jane had hit it.

Turning to us with large, watery eyes, Jake dropped to his knees. "Y-You hit her!" he shouted.

Just where the bullet—or *bullets*—had ended up was a mystery. I feared that Jane had gone too far, had shot to kill, and also that, upon her arrival to the body, she would deliver a coup de grace. When the two of us reached the Occupant, we both gasped in surprise.

It wasn't the Occupant we were looking at, but Elizabeth.

Crying and clutching at her calf, where a bullet had passed clean through, Elizabeth Morrissey looked up at us confusedly. She was weeping too much to speak, but for that moment, there was no visible trace of the Occupant in her.

"I'll be damned," blurted Jane, setting down her rifle and immediately thrusting her hands into the bag of rope. "Boys, hold her down!" she commanded.

Jake and I did as we were told. Using all of our strength, we gripped her wrists and ankles, holding them close together so that Jane could bind them with complicated knots. With great speed and zero hesitance, I watched Jane tie Elizabeth's arms and legs together several times over, the knots so tight, firm and intricate that I wondered if she wasn't a Green Beret. Elizabeth kept on sobbing the whole way through, said not a word, and was apparently too weak to resist us.

The final knot had been tied around her ankles when Elizabeth's body began to quake and change. Her eyes were the first to transform, going dark and then expanding till they looked like the hollows of trees. The roars of the dead erupted from her mouth as it unhinged, and her limbs, fighting suddenly against the restraints, looked on the verge of dislocating at the joints, such was the energy she put up in resistance.

But she was trapped.

For once, the predator had been restrained.

I stood up, staring down at the Occupant in awe as it

shook and spat. It was a sight to behold. "See?" I told Jane. "Elizabeth really is still in there. I told you."

Jake, despite his terror, was overjoyed at this discovery. "We can save her! We can do this!" he said. Then, looking to the serious wound on her leg, he grew visibly deflated. "That isn't going to kill her, is it?"

Jane shook her head. "No. Not right away, anyhow. Not while this thing is still living in her." She motioned to us both, giving us a cue to pick it up and carry it into the church. "We don't have a lot of time. Let's get her inside and do this."

Taking hold of the Occupant as though it were a rolled-up carpet, Jake and I ferried it into the church hastily and set it down between a pair of overturned pews. Having calmed somewhat, the specter looked up at each of us in turn. What was going through its head just then—what savage acts it was hoping to commit once freed—I didn't want to guess.

The transfer would involve me injuring the captive. I'd hit it in the head, punch or kick it, but would abstain from a killing blow. We had to test what amount of punishment the thing would be willing to take before abandoning Elizabeth's body. Once we'd figured out that limit, we'd have Jane, who was presently asking Jake to tie her arms and legs together with rope, invite the Occupant into her own body. There was no telling whether the spirit would take the bait, especially with Elizabeth so close by, but we hoped it would and planned to flee with Elizabeth at the first sign of success.

I picked up Jane's rifle and, as we'd discussed beforehand, struck the Occupant with the butt of it, right in the gut. The specter flinched, but to my surprise, Elizabeth didn't make a reappearance. Growling and fixing me in its black eyes, it remained unchanged. I focused next on its hands, bringing down the butt of the rifle against one of its fingers like a hammer. The digit could be heard to snap as it was sandwiched between the stock and the stone floor, and this blow *did* cause a change. The Occupant was overthrown, and when I looked down at its face again I saw Elizabeth staring back at me. She wailed in pain, closing her hand and trying to roll onto her side.

While all of this was going on, Jane had taken a seat on the floor. Her wrists had been tied, as had her ankles, and she had her eyes closed.

"Call out to it, Jane," I said, my hands growing sweaty as I gripped the rifle. I didn't want to hurt Elizabeth any more, didn't want to keep this torture session going. "Invite it in. Think back to those days in the cabin, to the chair. Your uncle would strap you in and you'd sit in the darkness, eyes and ears covered. You remember what it felt like, don't you? You remember sensing it in the room—seeing it, but not with your eyes. And then it would take hold of you. Speak through you. Try to remember."

I was talking out of my ass, hoping that this speech of mine would help her get into the proper mindset. Jane remained on the floor, eyes squeezed shut as though she were focusing on blocking me out, but didn't say a word.

Elizabeth's eyes began to change again. They were darkening. Her lips parted and from deep inside her there trickled the cries of the dead, escaping sporadically like a balloon leaking air. I was going to have to injure her again. It was all I could do to keep the Occupant from completely overtaking her. Gulping and steeling my resolve, I singled out another of her fingers and, raising the rifle over my head, ground it against the stone.

Lurching and spitting, the Occupant's malformed

features began to fade and Elizabeth's tear-dampened face came back into view. Jake was looking on in horror. Every time I moved to hit her, he had to fight the urge to snatch the gun away from me. He hesitated only because it looked to be having some effect. This time, when Elizabeth burst to the surface, he knelt beside her, cupped her aching hands in his, and tried to lend his support. "It's me, babe. We're going to help you, OK? Just hold on. Don't let it back in. I know you have it in you—fight! Don't let it inside."

Shaking with disgust, I let the gun droop to my side and looked to Jane, queasy. "J-Jane, I... I don't want to hit her again. Are you feeling anything?"

Jane Corvine met my gaze.

Her eyes were the color of India ink.

23

The transfer had worked.

So, looking into Jane's ebon eyes, why didn't I feel successful?

Her body hitched forward and she groaned like a spike of pain had just been driven through her midsection. Bucking against her restraints, she grit her teeth. Tears rolled down her cheeks, and when her mouth opened, I felt myself transported back in time.

Back at Corvine's cabin, I'd listened to his recordings of the Hiawatha sessions. I'd heard young *Janie's* protestations and crying jags on those tapes, and the voice I was now listening to in the abandoned church was eerily similar. Jane sobbed, "I can feel it... I can feel it inside of me again!" She sounded just like a little girl, and the knowledge that I'd bound her up and subjected her to this violation, like her uncle had done, made me ill. "It's in me again," she said, black eyes springing wide open and a torrent of tears seeping from their borders. "It's like... it's like it never left..."

At the same time, Elizabeth was staring up at the broken

roof of the church, trying to catch her breath. She'd said nothing since snapping out of her possessed state, and whenever she looked to Jake, still kneeling at her side, there wasn't much recognition in her gaze. I feared that maybe the Occupant's time in her had led to some atrophy of her mind —to some change we hadn't anticipated, but a few moments later, she coughed his name, "J-Jake?" and I felt a twinge of relief.

We'd managed to coerce the Occupant into Jane's body. There was only one thing left to do, and that was to run. Jake and I had discussed this part. We were to pick up Elizabeth and run as far from the church as our legs would allow. We knew, generally, that we had to head south, and Jane had given us her compass to use, suspecting that it would function again when the Occupant's presence was no longer so strong as to interfere with it.

Jane, who was currently bound up, was to try and keep the Occupant inside of her, distracted, until it finally fled her, as it always did during her sessions with her uncle. When the spirit left her body, unable to seize Elizabeth, who would be too far away by then, Jane would inch to a corner of the church, where Jake had hidden a folding knife that she could use to cut herself free of the rope. Once she'd done that, she'd be free to leave the woods as well. Provided that we all made it out, we planned to wait at her truck, or else make it to the nearest road and hitchhike to a local rest stop, where we'd meet up.

Filled with adrenaline and knowing that time was of the essence, I thanked Jane and moved to pick up Elizabeth. "You're doing great, Jane. Keep it inside of you, don't let it out. We're getting out of here."

Jake and I lifted Elizabeth, her body mostly limp. Even if

we'd cut her free, she'd have been too weak to walk on her own. Carrying her through the dense woods was going to be a logistical nightmare, and the three of us were going to get hurt plenty while trying to manage it. But it didn't matter. When we'd secured a tight hold on her, we started for the door.

And I would have made it all the way outside then if I hadn't heard Jane suddenly coughing.

She hacked terribly, like her lungs were about to burst out of her mouth, and then her coughing turned into choking.

I blanched, looking to Jake. "Something's wrong with Jane," I said.

He didn't look back, but instead picked up his pace, dragging me through the door. "Doesn't matter, we need to go," he said.

I couldn't do that, and he knew it. I stopped in my tracks, lowering Elizabeth's legs to the ground. "Can you carry her on your own?" I asked. "At least, for a little while? I need to make sure she's all right."

Jake eyed me sternly. He didn't want to slow down for anything, to risk losing Elizabeth again, and I couldn't blame him. But I also couldn't let Jane suffer after all she'd done for us. I ignored him, returning to the church and dropping down beside Jane, who was writhing on the floor, the veins in her neck sticking way out.

"Jane!" I shouted. "What's the matter? Are you all right? Breathe!" I tried to sit her up, but her body was thrashing too terribly. A sucking sound, as of air trying to get past some sort of bolus trapped in her throat, could be heard with her every attempt to breathe. She was choking on something, but I couldn't say what. Scrambling for a flashlight, I wrenched her mouth open with one hand and tried to take a look at her throat, hoping I'd be able to pluck out whatever was blocking her airway. "Damn it," I said, fussing over the flashlight. "Stay with me, Jane. I'm no good at the Heimlich."

Finally, the flashlight came on, and I was able to take a look inside of Jane's mouth. The gold crowns on her molars threw back some of the light, and a moment's glance told me her mouth was clear. Deeper down, though, at the entrance to her throat, just behind her uvula, I could see something.

It was narrow and fleshy.

And it was *moving.*

I jerked away from her in disgust. Taking another glance into her throat, and supporting Jane's lolling head on my arm, I found several moving objects coming up out of her throat.

They were fingers, and they all belonged to the same hand.

Three, then four digits eased through the channel of soft tissue comprising her throat, all of them vying to burst out of her mouth. I jumped back, letting her hit the ground, and crawled so that I bumped into the edge of the doorway. Jake eyed me with annoyance from outside. "What are you doing in there? We need to hurry up!"

Suddenly, Jane sat up, but not of her own volition. As though she had another body somehow stowed away in her frame, something inside of her was calling the shots, thrusting her into a seated position. Her eyes, huge and pitch-colored, turned to study me, and a smile graced her lips. "*Didn't you know?*" asked the Occupant from inside her body. Her lips weren't moving. "*I never wanted this one.*"

Jane's entire body began to shake. Though bound at the limbs, she managed to fall to one side and then inch across the floor towards me like a worm. Convulsing all the while, whimpering, Jane had come within three feet of me when a dark liquid began to run in thick streams from her eyes, ears and nose.

Blood.

Her pale face illuminated by the moonlight drifting in from the church entrance, she stared up at me with her black eyes, cheeks stained in blood. And then—with a final cry—she lowered her head till her face met the floor. Jane grew still.

I knew Jane Corvine was dead before I even reached out to nudge her. I tried picking her up, shaking her, but nothing I did could reignite the spark of life that'd just gone out in her eyes. Rolling her over, I saw—with no little horror —that her eyes had returned to normal. The Occupant, having destroyed her, had left her body.

No sooner did I note the change in Jane's eyes did I hear a ruckus outside the church. Jake yelped, and something else—an animal, I thought—howled in anger.

I staggered out into the moonlight and watched as Elizabeth's eyes went dark.

She wasn't Elizabeth anymore.

Jake had let go of her, and had fallen to the ground. "W-What..." When he became sure that the Occupant still couldn't break out of its restraints—though for how long that would be the case was impossible to say—he looked up at me with unveiled fury. "Why did you stop? Why did you have to turn back?"

I glanced down at the Occupant and the damned thing looked up at me in return. There was something knowing in its gaze, something of satisfaction in having foiled our plot and killed Jane. "Jane is dead," I muttered. "It killed her."

Jake paused, but his anger rose to the fore again within an instant. "That's... that's not my problem!" he shouted. "We were supposed to get Elizabeth out of here while she was tied up in the church! We had a plan, professor. We had a plan!" His face was red, and his lips were dripping now with spittle. He fought his way to a standing position and jabbed a finger at me. "You did this. You let it back into her! We should have followed the plan, professor!"

I was feeling a lot of things in that moment. Jake was right, of course. Maybe, just maybe, if I'd stayed with him and helped him get Elizabeth away from the church, we would have saved her. I felt immense guilt, too, for what had happened to Jane. She'd spent her entire adult life running from the shadows of her past, and because I'd dragged her back into this madness she'd died at the hands of the very thing that had hounded her. The Occupant had done it, but the blood was on my hands. Everything that had happened in these woods could in some way be traced back to my involvement. If I'd never taken part, if I'd never come here, then all of us could have been safe, could have gone on living.

But for all the sadness and guilt I felt, I still hadn't lost sight of the mission.

There was still a job to do.

"You're right," I said, "and I'm sorry, Jake. We had a plan. It didn't work. So," I continued, drawing my gun, "it's time that we follow plan-B."

There was no alternative left to us. Elizabeth Morrissey had to die. I took no joy in the act of killing, would regret it till my dying day, but I knew it had to be done. Like W. R. Corvine and Jamieson Monroe before me, this was my mission, my one chance to set things right. Corvine, having realized his terrible mistakes, had killed his patient, Enid, and had hoped to find a permanent solution to the problem of the Occupant before his death. Jamieson Monroe, having learned about the true nature of the Lancaster curse, had come back to Milsbourne, seeking to murder every descendant of that cursed line he could find—not because he was a bloodthirsty savage, but because, like me, he'd understood his responsibility to the human race.

I pointed the gun at the Occupant. From this range, I couldn't miss. Hot tears filled my eyes, blurring my vision. The specter, knowing what was coming, tried to move, tried to roll away, but I pinned it to the ground with my foot. "Elizabeth, I'm sorry," I said.

I pulled the trigger.

But not before Jake managed to step in front of me and clock me across the jaw.

I fell to the ground, my eyes rolling into the back of my head as I strained to hold onto consciousness. Teeth had been loosened by that blow, and I could taste blood welling in my cheek, where my molars had dug in. Jake was a big guy, a whole head taller than me, and he hit like one. My body told me to move, that I needed to get up and defend myself against the blow that must surely be coming. But I was too slow. The punch had left me dazed and I could hardly even sit up.

That was when I noticed it.

I'd dropped the damn gun.

Looking around dizzily, patting the grass as though I were looking for a lost contact lens, I tried to find the firearm. Expecting Jake to pounce on me at any moment, I looked upward and focused my blurry vision just ahead, where I found him kneeling beside the Occupant. The

Occupant, thank Christ, was still tied up, right where I'd left it. I wasn't sure if my bullet had hit the mark.

When I could finally stand without feeling like I'd black out, I located the gun, which had fallen into a patch of tall grass near the church's memorial plaque, and then approached the pair cautiously to examine my work.

The result was not at all what I'd expected.

There was a rapidly-growing pool of blood between Jake and the Occupant, but to my horror, I soon saw it wasn't coming from the latter.

Jake, in his haste to keep me from firing, had taken the bullet. It'd run through his thigh, leaving a nice, big hole in his jeans from which blood freely gurgled. The Occupant, like a black-eyed cat, had managed to roll onto its stomach, and was excitedly lapping up the blood from the grass. I felt my knees go weak, and I fell for a second time as I watched Jake grimace through the pain. "J-Jake..."

He looked up at me, clutching his leg, and simply shook his head. The blood flow didn't slow in the least. One couldn't survive a shot like that, certainly not all the way out here in the wilderness. I'd probably gotten him in the femoral artery. His entire blood supply would end up in the grass within minutes.

I got up, motioned to the church, where we'd stashed all of our supplies. "I'll... I'll get the first aid kit..."

He winced, doubled over so that his face met the bloodied grass. When he looked up at me next, he looked every bit the demon as his girlfriend, his face running crimson. Summoning up his remaining strength, he managed to stand—which only increased the flow—and charged at me like a rampaging gorilla. "You... you did this! You did *all* of this!" He belted me with a blood-soaked fist and I crumpled to the ground. I made no effort to stop him, to defend myself. I was too stunned, and besides, I knew in my heart that I deserved it. He was right to hate me, to blame me, to kill me, if he so chose.

Jake reared up to kick me but lost his balance. He fell flat onto his back and I knew then that he'd never get back up. His chest heaving, he stared up at the moon, cursing me. I apologized to him repeatedly, but if he heard me he made no sign. After a while, his chest no longer moved, and his lips ceased their curses.

That left me and the Occupant.

They say misery loves company, and the Occupant was misery incarnate. Not a moment after the life had gone from Jake, I heard the specter loose a throaty chuckle. The very sound cut through my gut-churning sadness and roused in me a profound anger. I marched over to the thing and, wiping the tears from my eyes, pointed the gun right at it. "This ends here," I said, squeezing the trigger.

There was a click.

A quiet, impotent click.

I studied the gun in surprise, stupefied, and then tried pulling the trigger again. And again. It wouldn't fire.I racked the slide. Still nothing. I'd run out of ammo.

The Occupant laughed again. "*I guess it doesn't end here,*" came the voice from below me. "*It never ends.*"

I cast the gun away and marched back into the church, where I took up the folding knife we'd hid for Jane's use. Pulling it open, I rushed back to the Occupant and wondered where best to plunge it. The black-eyed thing stared at me, as if it knew I didn't have the stones to slice Elizabeth's throat. Killing with a gun was relatively easy. You could do it from a distance; point and click. To use a knife, one had to get up-close and personal. I brandished the knife, toyed with the idea of sticking the specter in the heart, but ultimately put it away. "You're coming with me," I said. We're going to end this in the hills, like the people of this town did the last time you reared your head."

The Occupant did not move to resist me as I took hold of its arms and began to drag it away from the church. But it did speak. From behind me, its words wormed their way into my ear. "*It never ends,*" it reminded me.

24

I knew I was on the right path when the rows of cabins came into view. Dragging my captive behind me like a bag of cement, I trudged through woods and clearings alike. The Occupant didn't make a sound, didn't fight me. I supposed that it could have summoned up a boiling rain to scald me had it wanted to, but it didn't. This, I theorized, was due to some kind of spiritual tiredness on its part—or else it was a party trick it only liked to break out once every century. The entity had been through a lot—it had been forced to shift between two different bodies that night, and had been chased out of Elizabeth on more than one occasion due to our meddling. It had seemingly accepted its fate.

Or else it was planning something.

We left the cabins behind and began ascending the hills I knew to lead to the mines. Passing weathered equipment, small outcroppings of rock, the fog came rolling in and remained stuck in dense patches wherever the ground dipped. The moon was high, had grown brighter since our time outside the church, almost as though it'd come a little closer to the Earth to watch me out of curiosity.

"What is it you want?" I asked, slowing just a bit as the climb tired me out. I hefted the Occupant up the hill like a slab of beef and then continued dragging it by the wrists when I'd sufficiently recovered. "Why are you doing this? Why are you even in this world of ours?"

The specter didn't respond, except to study me with its obsidian eyes.

I dragged it further, reaching hilltops that sprouted formations of jagged rock. We were getting close. Finding the mineshaft where Sarah Lancaster had met her end would be difficult, but at that moment I'd have settled for any old shaft.

Now and then, I'd hear harsh whispers issuing from inside the thing. The dead were a chattery bunch this night. I tried not to let it get to me, to ignore it, and continued hiking through the hills in search of the mineshaft I'd discovered previously.

My arms ached, felt on the verge of disconnecting from my body, when I finally stumbled upon it. The fog was thick there, but the brightness of the moon lit up the hollows of the pit and brought to light the sun-bleached bones I'd glimpsed my first time round. Pulling the Occupant to the edge of this aperture, I sighed, yanking the knife from my back pocket and opening it. It was a sizable blade, rather sharp, but I hadn't decided yet on how to use it. The thought of carving into a living thing—even so despicable a monstrosity as this one—sent shivers through me.

The Occupant seemed to know it, because staring up at me from the circling fog below, it chuckled. *"You haven't got the stones to carve up the girl."*

This moment was thirty years—no, more than a *hundred* years—in the making. Every move I'd made since I'd decided to visit Chaythe Asylum had led to this. If I could only summon up the courage, I would be returning the Occupant to the place where Joseph Lancaster had first encountered it more than a century and a half ago. I squeezed the knife in my hand and stared down at the captive.

"*Why fight it?*" asked the Occupant? "*You should let me devour you. Untie me, and I'll put you out of your misery. It never ends, so why fight it?*"

I was tired of hearing its voice. "Shut up," I said. "I'm sending you back to where you came from."

The thing stared up at me, unblinking. "*You would kill the girl? No, not you. You don't have it in you.*"

My gaze drifted to the Occupant's side, where I'd managed to shoot it the night before. Studying its flesh, I found the wound had mostly healed. That didn't seem possible, but then the parasitical entity probably worked hard at keeping its host alive. Only a mortal injury would be too difficult to mend. If I was going to do this, then I'd have to go all the way—make it so that the Occupant could never heal and use this body again.

I dropped to my knees, shaking. Placing one hand atop the Occupant's head and holding it still, I took the knife firmly in my grasp. "Elizabeth, if you're in there, then I want you to know I'm sorry. I'm sorry for everything. I don't want to do this, but I have to set you free."

The ragged edges of its mouth drooping open, the Occupant replied, "*She can't hear you. She's with me. They're all with me.*"

It was time.

Overriding my brain's order to stop, to second-guess things, I plunged the knife into the Occupant's throat. Almost immediately, the black eyes and serpent-like maw vanished and Elizabeth Morrissey came to the surface. But there wasn't time to dwell on that. I had to keep going—to hesitate would only prolong her suffering. Warm blood sprang from the new wound, dousing my hands, spraying the rocks.

The blade caught on the thicker bits of her anatomy—the windpipe, certain of the muscles in the throat—but I cleaved through them while screaming at the top of my lungs, and didn't stop hacking until I'd broken through the brainstem, severing the head in its entirety. I didn't dare look at it with any closeness. I merely looked at the neck-down, made sure I'd desecrated the body so that the spirit could never take hold of it again.

It was done.

It was finally done.

I let go of Elizabeth's orange hair and let the head roll over the lip of the chasm, where it bounced to the very bottom. Then, barely able to see straight and my pulse nearly shooting out of my temples, I gave the twitching body a shove into the pit. Elizabeth came to rest in a nest of bleached bones. Eventually, the scavengers would get to her, and her bones would become indistinguishable from the rest at the bottom of that shaft.

Blubbering, I lost all control of my gag reflex and threw up on the ground, heaving until I was dizzy. I then fell onto my side, eyes stinging with wave after wave of tears. How long I remained in that position, I really can't say. It must have been several minutes. Or maybe a couple of hours passed. I couldn't move, couldn't think, and my mind and body suffered a kind of schism as I tried to rationalize what I'd done.

When I finally felt it in myself to move, to distance myself from the pit which now reeked of blood, I felt completely detached from my body. Staring down at my hands, still sticky with her blood, they didn't look like my own. The first shuffling steps I took from the lip of the mineshaft were unsteady, like I'd have to teach myself to walk all over again. My eyes and throat burned for all the tears I'd shed, but now my expression slumped into pure vacancy.

Jane Corvine was dead—killed by the very thing she'd feared most.

Both Jake and Elizabeth were dead as well. When I'd first gotten to know them, they'd approached me because they'd wanted me to show them ghosts. Both had died by my hand in these silent woods. Maybe, I thought, the two of them would become ghosts themselves, and wound wander these hills together till the end of the world.

The Occupant, for all intents and purposes, was a spirit left to wander the forest in search of a new host—a Lancaster—that it would probably never find again.

I'd learned the fate of the enigmatic Dr. Corvine. I'd uncovered the truth about the whereabouts of scholar Jamieson Monroe. I'd amassed an enviable amount of knowledge about the widely-reported Third Ward Incident, and had pieced together the history of abandoned Milsbourne, Michigan—things you couldn't find in any history books.

And now, I was alone. Truly alone. All of the knowledge, all of the intrigue, all of the relationships meant nothing anymore. The plot had run its course and the players had all taken a bow. This was how it ended, I supposed.

I marched into the fog, following the sloping of the hills.

25

My remaining time in the Michigan woods was a blur. I took something of a tour of ruin, revisiting places I'd previously been. I walked by the cabin where Paul Coleman had met his end, and then found my way to the church, where Jake remained on his back, undisturbed, staring eternally at the twinkling stars. I stepped past Jane's body, rifling through the remainder of our rations and loading everything useful into a single pack. I went through her things, took her smokes and remaining cash, and then left the church behind. From there, I passed the clearing where we'd made our camp, spied the warped blue tent that flapped in the wind as if to wave goodbye.

I emptied out the first aid kit and had a look at what it contained. There was a bottle of rubbing alcohol, which I emptied over my busted lip and numerous bumps and scratches. I chewed up seven or eight Acetaminophen tablets and chased them with a swish and spit of hydrogen peroxide, which I hoped would help keep the inside of my cut-up mouth from getting infected.

A compass is surprisingly easy to use. I followed the needle, went south, and finally found my way to a paved road by early afternoon the next day. The thing had worked like a charm, hadn't malfunctioned the way it had when the Occupant had been on the prowl. I walked along that road for several miles. Eventually, a fidgeting truck driver who was probably hopped up on meth and looking for some road head came by and asked if I needed a lift. I pretended not to hear him and he drove off. An hour later, a pair of kids in a Volkswagen, having just wrapped up a camping trip of their own, offered to give me a ride as far as Detroit.

I took them up on it and probably said all of two words the whole way there. After sleeping in their back seat most of the way, I handed them a few bucks and said, "thank you" as they offloaded me at a Detroit Denny's.

I'M NOT LOOKING for your pity, your forgiveness. I know what kind of man I am. I know what I did, and I'll live with it the rest of my life. Maybe you'd have handled things differently —would have walked a higher path. Well, congratulations on being so goddamn virtuous. You're above reproach, aren't you? Me? I did what I had to do to prevent further loss, further calamity.

It's easy to act outraged, to balk at the barbarity of my actions. But when push comes to shove, it's much harder to act. Need I remind you, I didn't choose to end up in those woods. I was led. I'd been used, manipulated from afar by that damned Occupant. When the end came, I simply did what I had to do, like Corvine and Monroe before me. I put an end to it.

No, I never told anyone about what happened. How could I? Calling the authorities and letting them know about what had gone on in those woods would have only brought attention to the region, and in case you forgot, the Occupant, in some form or another, was still out there. It was better to let sleeping dogs lie, I decided. It wasn't for fear of being punished that I kept my lips shut—frankly, a lethal injection sounds mighty fine to me, most days—I didn't blab because it was the safest thing.

Maybe you're wondering what happened after I returned to civilization, or maybe you're one of those who wrote me off as a murderer, a piece of human garbage unworthy of your headspace. Well, for the curious, I'll tell you up front that things weren't pretty for me when I got back. I spent some days on the road, hitchhiking, and lost my already precarious teaching position at Moorlake University. That's right—the cheap-asses in the administration would have to find some other chump to teach those kids about Chaucer.

There were some questions. Elizabeth's parents got ahold of me at one point. I don't know how. They reached out to the administration and got my email address shortly before I was shit-canned, I supposed. They wrote to me, concerned because they hadn't seen or heard from their daughter since Jake and I had been by their house that night some weeks before. They wanted to know if I knew anything about their whereabouts. I wrote them back, crafting a real nice message about how young people sometimes run off together, and that, wherever they were, I felt sure they were together and happy. I like to think that it wasn't a complete lie.

Shortly thereafter, I couldn't afford to pay my rent and got evicted. I pawned most of my stuff and cashed out standing favors with friends and acquaintances in northwest Ohio. For almost two months, I couch-surfed.

I was down in the Columbus area, staying with a college buddy of mine, Alex, who taught biology at a private university. Tired of seeing me on his sofa, he offered to put in a good word for me at the university—Chapel Institute of Columbus—and even helped me spice up my resume with all kinds of outrageous power talk. After an awkward interview, where I barely held it together, I somehow ended up with a job. I was set to teach full time English. They had a shortage of instructors in their English department and were desperate to bring me on board. Their benefits package was far more comprehensive than the non-existent package at Moorlake U, and I signed on in a heartbeat.

I worked small jobs through the summer, saving up enough for my own apartment and eventually moving out of Alex's place, and then, in late August, started my first term at the Chapel Institute. Things were looking up. For the first time in my adult life, I had a real job, with real benefits. There were stirrings of a social life, too.

Though the months previous had been incredibly hard for me and I still couldn't sleep without a light on, I told myself that all of that—the Occupant, Milsbourne, the asylum, were in the past. That part of my life was over. I'd turned a new page, was ready to live a quiet life and make amends for the transgressions of my past. There were times along the way where I thought I felt those now familiar eyes staring out at me from some unseen abyss; where I found myself in an empty room and could have sworn that someone had only just been there. There were times when the memories had sharp teeth and took a bite out of me and left me curled up in bed for days, waiting for something to emerge from the shadows. I told myself all of that was behind me. That it hadn't been real.

I was wrong.

It never ends.

I'm afraid there's more to tell.

26

M y first semester at the Chapel Institute went by without so much as a hiccough.

I got my own office and didn't have to share it with the likes of patronizing, dandruff-ridden Phil. The pay was good, and no students came up to me after lectures to ask me about heading their extracurriculars.

Also, over the course of that first semester, I did something that I'd never much bothered with while teaching back in Moorlake. I got to know my fellow teachers. The other folks in the English department were friendly and happened to be close to me in age. There was Dylan, a creative writing teacher who'd had several stories published in impressive mags like *Glitter Train* and *The New Yorker*. There was Tanya, an instructor who happened to be married to the vice dean of the university and who brought in boxes of primo cupcakes from a bakery in downtown Columbus every Monday and Friday. There was Gerald, a former college athlete who'd torn his ACL and lost out on his chance to go pro, and who now taught Comp. 1 and

Comp. 2 classes while going out every other night to binge drink at clubs with girls young enough to be his daughters.

And then there was Rose.

Rose Dennings, a freckled brunette just an inch or two shorter than me, who looked something like a *Friends*-era Courtney Cox, was an associate professor who taught a couple of random poetry and lit courses. Her office was right next to mine, so I'd gotten to know her right from the get-go. She was something of a gossip, had been working at Chapel for just over two years, and knew everything there was to know about the area—from the best campus restaurants to the best places in Columbus to catch a cheap matinee.

One day, early in the semester when I was still struggling to put my old life behind me, she offered to show me around town. We both had the day off and took a cab into Columbus, enjoying a lunch, taking a shuttle to a large mall and then catching a movie. One thing led to another and she ended up spending the night at my new apartment. This became a regular occurrence, and before too long we were the office "item", a couple cooed at by the others in the English department.

Rose was unlike any other girl I'd ever dated. I'd broken off my last relationship before moving to Moorlake, not wanting to do the long distance thing, and hadn't really connected with anyone there. But from the moment I met Rose—please excuse the cliche—I knew she was different. A whole new breed of woman. We had similar tastes in books and music. Though she loved a good time out on the town, she was just as content to be a homebody, spending a day watching movies on the couch. She drank beer, didn't bother me on the daily to shave, and it's fair to say I fell head over heels for her. Things moved pretty quickly. Our passion flared. By the end of the fall semester, we were talking about the possibility of moving in together.

And so the pieces of a normal, happy life began to fall into place for me. I taught my classes, enjoyed bantering with my co-workers, and spent my evenings with Rose. Some nights, after making love, we'd sit up for hours talking. She'd tell me about her childhood, or about the traveling she'd done during her gap year. Sometimes, looking to me with real curiosity, she'd ask me about my past, about the teaching post I'd held previously and about why I'd moved to Columbus in the first place.

One thing I wasn't ready to do—that I would never be able to do, honestly—was open up to her about my past. Oh, sure, I told her about my upbringing, clear through my own college years, but my time spent teaching at Moorlake U was always a blank spot, something I'd conveniently glaze over. She meant no harm in it, was genuinely curious about my past, but even I didn't care to reflect on those days. They were too fresh, too new, even then. Some nights, when I dreamt, I could still picture the scenery of Chaythe Asylum, or the abandoned buildings of Milsbourne, along with the people I'd explored them with, now deceased.

I wished I could open up to her, but the horrors of those days would be my cross to bear till I drew my last breath. No one could know—the knowledge was dangerous. And anyway, it was all too unbelievable for someone who hadn't actually been involved. Had someone told me about the Occupant before all of this began—about half the shit I'd witnessed back in Moorlake—I wouldn't have believed them. It was simply easier to deflect back to her. "Tell me more about your childhood, your family," I'd say, and after a flash of disappointment, she'd talk about herself.

I learned during one such discussion that her family hailed from Michigan originally. "What part?" I asked.

She had her head pressed to my bare chest and had been caught up in listening to my heartbeat. "The Upper Peninsula," she said. "It's really beautiful up there—lots of trees. Good fishing, since you're on the Great Lakes. Ever been?"

I paused, not knowing how to react. I'd been to the Upper Peninsula, all right. I knew a thing or two about these many trees she was talking about, and I couldn't really recommend them. "You don't say..."

She sensed my discomfort and gave me a pleading look.

"Yeah," I admitted. "I've been there. Once. Don't have any plans to go back, though. Let's just say I have a lot of bad memories about the place."

Not long after that, Rose got dressed and set out, having some appointment in the morning that she couldn't be late for. I spent the remainder of the night alone in bed, staring at the ceiling, the lights in my bedroom all on, contemplating my past. I felt an immense guilt for any joy I'd managed to cultivate since moving to Columbus.

Jane Corvine didn't get to experience any joy. Not anymore. Neither did Jake or Elizabeth. Not after what I'd done to them.

I wondered, yet again, whether I'd ever be able to put this behind me, or at least not flinch at the very mention of the State of Michigan.

～

THE FALL SEMESTER ENDED. Everything outside of the occasional bad dream was blissful for me. A month-long winter break was on its way. Rose and I spent a good deal of time together during the first two weeks of the vacation, and then she started preparing for a trip to her parents' place in Dayton where she'd spend the holidays. Around the 20th of December, as she was getting ready to depart on her trip, I invited her to my place for one last night of Chinese takeout and Netflix. I wouldn't see her again till early January, but we promised to chat daily.

It was snowing that night, I remember. It was a faint snow, the kind that doesn't stick, but which falls in really fat, impressive flakes like something in an old Christmas-themed painting. I'd given her my gift, a poorly-wrapped bottle of her favorite perfume and a snowman-patterned scarf that'd caught her eye at a downtown boutique. She'd picked up a handful of vinyl records to go with the turntable I'd recently treated myself to—Sinatra's *In The Wee Small Hours* and others that were near and dear to me.

After a farewell romp in the sheets, the two of us sat up in my bedroom, relaxing, and she got that thoughtful look in her eyes like she wanted to launch into one of our long discussions. To my surprise, she kissed me on the lips and said, "Hey, I've been wondering about something. Those 'bad memories' you've got about Michigan. What are they? Did you teach up in Michigan or something?"

The question took me by surprise and I gave a very obvious deflection. "Ah, it was nothing. It's just not my kind of place, you know. Like you said... lots of trees. I'm a city boy, through and through. Never been much for nature." I turned the tables. "How about you? Did you like living in Michigan?" I asked.

She shrugged, giving me a half-smile. "Well, it's funny, but I hardly remember it. My parents and I moved out of there when I was still very young. In fact, I don't know the full story behind it, but whenever my dad has talked about it in the past, I get the impression that we didn't leave—but were run out. Maybe it was a debt-related thing, I don't know. We even changed our last name. I think it must have been a legal problem, but my dad doesn't like to talk about it."

"Oh?" I asked. "What was your last name before 'Dennings', then?"

"We used to be the Lancasters," she replied.

The pre-bedroom wine I'd enjoyed crept up my throat and I felt a tightness in my chest. The look on my face must have been terrible, because Rose sat up and looked at me with concern.

"Are you OK?" she asked.

I ran a hand across my face, sighed. "Yeah, yeah. Of course. I'm just... kind of tired," I said, cracking an unconvincing smile. If she'd still had her head on my chest, listened to my heart, she'd have called my bluff, because at that moment it was racing.

"OK," she said. "I'll put out the lights."

I stopped her. "No, no... just lay with me," I said, pulling her back into bed. I held her close. My insistence on sleeping with at least one light on was one thing that always bothered her about staying at my place. Tonight, though, she didn't put up any fuss and as I held her close, I heard her drift off within minutes.

I wasn't afforded the luxury of an easy sleep, however. I was wide awake.

If Rose was to be believed—and I had no reason to doubt her—her father had been a Lancaster who had lived in the Upper Peninsula of Michigan, and who'd been run out under strange circumstances. I didn't know the full details, and neither did Rose, but I remembered something Paul Coleman had told me during my time in Milsbourne, when he'd regaled me with the story of the Lancaster curse. He'd claimed that certain of the Lancasters, not feeling safe in Milsbourne and often shunned by the other local families, had fled from the region. Some had even changed their names. That Rose's father checked all of those boxes was one hell of a coincidence.

At this point in my life, I knew a thing or two about coincidences.

A true coincidence is a lot rarer than people know. More often than not, things merely have the appearance of coincidence, when in fact there's someone silently pulling strings behind the scenes, arranging for a particular outcome. One spring day, not so very long ago, I'd watched a kid in downtown Moorlake die in a hit and run accident and had, shortly thereafter, gotten rolled up into Elizabeth Morrissey's ghost hunting club, which led us to Chaythe Asylum...

The Occupant had used me as a pawn in the past—a pawn that would deliver it a female in the Lancaster line— without my even realizing it. Was that what was happening now? Or was I simply reading too deeply into things, psyching myself out? I tried to sleep, told myself it was nothing, and repeated, again and again, that all of that supernatural business was in the past, that I needn't concern myself with it. I'd put a stop to the Occupant back in Michigan by committing an unspeakable sin. The entity, if it still existed in this world at all, had returned to its nightly wanderings of the unpeopled Michigan woods and was no longer a direct threat.

Eventually, I drifted into an uneasy sleep. The lights in the room didn't help beat back the specters leering from the borders of my memories, though.

27

Rose got dressed and set out around eight in the morning. She was hesitant to leave, but not wanting to keep her parents waiting, she prepared for her two hour drive and promised to call me once she got there safe and sound. I followed her to the door, gave her a kiss and watched her as she walked out to her Volvo. When she'd gone, I locked up and decided to catch up on my reading. I had a stack of novels a foot high that I'd been hurting to read and a bottle of decent scotch in the cabinet that I'd been saving for just such an occasion.

The next two days went by in a blur of booze, books and greasy delivery food. Since moving to Columbus, I'd given up my smoking habit. Affording packs of smokes—even the crappier brands—is hard to do when you're jobless, and all of the people I'd crashed with after my eviction had been pretty staunch anti-smokers. So, I'd quit cold turkey. I didn't even crave the cigarettes a whole lot anymore, but when the itch came, usually when I was drinking, I'd treat myself to the occasional smoke. A friend had introduced me to a cigar shop in town from which I'd purchased a couple of Nat

Sherman cigars, and I lit up while paging through an excellent techno-thriller.

Something occurred to me towards the end of that second day, however. Rose had never called to let me know she'd made it safely to her parents' place. I didn't think much of it. It'd sounded like her parents intended to keep her busy over the break, with luncheons and shopping trips, and I was sure she'd simply forgotten. Picking up my phone, I tapped out a quick text, asking her how she was doing, and left it at that.

Or, at least, I'd intended to.

A phone chirped somewhere in my apartment, startling me. I looked down at my own, and when I was sure it wasn't the culprit, I got up and started searching. The chirp—the ringer Rose always used—sounded again a few minutes later. I shuffled from room to room and singled out the source of the chirping. It was coming from my bedroom. Specifically, from underneath my bed. I pulled away the bedskirt and discovered Rose's purse tucked neatly beneath the frame.

"Oh, crap," I muttered. She'd forgotten her purse. No wonder she hadn't called.

I set it on top of the bed and wondered why she hadn't come back for it. It was likely she'd driven a long while before noticing she'd forgotten it, and she'd probably thought it safe in my care until she returned. I considered the possibility of my running it to her parents' place. If nothing else, it would make for a convenient excuse to see her again. The drive to Dayton wasn't so far that it would be a lot of trouble, and the weather was looking decent.

The only trouble was that I didn't know her parents' address. Carrying the purse over to my laptop, I pulled up a browser window and fed "Dennings Dayton Ohio" into

The Occupant 189

Google. The first page was full of different hits featuring addresses, phone numbers and more.

But near the top of the page, hosted by what looked to be a Dayton news site, was something that caught my eye. I clicked on the link, which led to a news item less than a day old, entitled DAYTON COUPLE MISSING, FOUL PLAY SUSPECTED.

The story, a brief writeup, detailed an ongoing investigation into the very recent disappearances of Bradley and Gloria Dennings, residents of Dayton, Ohio. Investigators were alerted to the scene by a neighbor who'd noted a disturbance the night before. Upon their arrival to the scene, authorities reportedly found traces of blood around the property, as well as a good deal of damage to the interior of the house. The couple, in their early 60's, were not found and were presumed missing.

I closed out of the tab and shut my laptop, my blood turning to ice. Were these two missing people in Dayton Rose's parents? Where had they gone? Surely this had simply been some kind of Christmastime break-in gone wrong? I told myself it was just a coincidence. Just another weird coincidence, nothing more.

But at the back of my mind, I began to suspect it was anything but a coincidence.

I considered the possibility that this was the most recent incarnation of the Lancaster curse. I pictured Rose, entering her parents' home the night before, her eyes black, her mouth unhinged. I imagined her tearing them apart, feasting on their blood. I thought I could hear the voices of the dead as my heater kicked on and my hands began to tremble. I sucked down two fingers' worth of scotch to get my head straight.

My curiosity getting the better of me, I dove into Rose's

purse, wondering if I wouldn't be able to find something related to her parents inside. Maybe her parents weren't named Bradley and Gloria—maybe this incident in Dayton was completely unrelated to her, I told myself. Emptying the contents of the purse onto my desk, I was surprised at how little there was to sift through. Aside from the hair scrunchies and bobby pins that clattered out, I found a white clamshell of birth control pills, her cellphone, a pack of gum and a smattering of old receipts and movie ticket stubs. There was one other thing as well—a slip of folded paper that'd been lining the bottom.

I had a look at everything, starting with the birth control pills. The fact that the circle of pills, a month's supply, was completely intact did not escape my notice. She hadn't taken a single one in the past twenty-odd days. Why was that? She was over at my apartment every other night, would surely end up pregnant seeing as how we didn't use any other form of protection. Setting the pills aside, I picked up the folded sheet of paper and opened it.

It turned out to be a handwritten note, something, I wagered, she'd expected me to find. The message on it, written very neatly so as not to be misread, was comprised of only two lines.

Two lines I'd read before.

I stared at that note a long while. Before I knew it, a stray tear had fallen from my cheek and stained the page, blurring the ink. My hands shook, and I knew that the entire bottle of scotch would not steady them. Crushing the note within my palm, I slumped in my chair and wept.

In 1989, shortly before his death, W. R. Corvine had written a cryptic note, a sort of warning, and had left it behind in a box beneath the floorboards of his cabin in Michigan. The note, written in Rose's distinct hand, replicated the last two lines of the doctor's missive, forever burned in my memory, and solidified something I should have realized long ago.

The door has been opened.

It's already too late.

And of course, she was right.

THANK YOU FOR READING!

Thank you for reading!

I hope you've enjoyed **The Occupant**. If you'd like to know about my future work the moment it's released, join my mailing list at the link below!

Please consider leaving a review for this book. Your reviews are invaluable to me; they help me to hone my craft and help new readers find my books.

Subscribe to Ambrose Ibsen's newsletter here:
    http://eepurl.com/bovafj

ABOUT THE AUTHOR

Once upon a time, a young Ambrose Ibsen discovered a collection of ghost stories on his father's bookshelf. He was never the same again.

Apart from horror fiction, he enjoys good coffee, brewed strong.

For more information:
ambroseibsen.com
admin@ambroseibsen.com

CPSIA information can be obtained
at www.ICGtesting.com
Printed in the USA
LVHW09s1214190818
587437LV00002B/550/P